THE LAST NOEL

HEATHER GRAHAM

THE LAST NOEL

MIRA®

ISBN-13: 978-0-7783-2525-3
ISBN-10:   0-7783-2525-3

THE LAST NOEL

www.MIRABooks.com

Printed in U.S.A.

First Printing: November 2007
10 9 8 7 6 5 4 3 2 1

PROLOGUE

"But...this is *Christmas Eve!*"

The old man, frail and almost skeletally thin, stared at them in disbelief. His voice was tremulous, and he seemed to shake like a delicate, wind-blown leaf.

"You're right. It *is* Christmas Eve, old-timer, and you're not supposed to be here," Scooter said.

Craig found that he couldn't speak. This wasn't supposed to happen. There shouldn't have been anyone here. When he'd hooked up with Scooter Blane, the man had been all but invisible. He and his partner, Quintin Lark, were becoming heroes in a certain stratum of underworld society for their long string of extremely profitable robberies. But no one had ever gotten hurt. Ever.

But they only hit places that were empty.

Like this place should have been today.

There had been rumors, though. Rumors that the pair could be ruthless when they chose. But rumors were just rumors. Crooks needed them, went out of their way to create them, because they lived and died for them.

Killed for them?

But the real word on the street was that the pair were experts at slipping in and slipping out. Hitting fast, disappearing.

As far as Craig had been aware, they had never hurt anyone or even, thanks to careful planning, come across anyone still working during one of their heists.

He had discovered when he threw in with them that Scooter was frighteningly savvy with electronics. He'd seen that demonstrated when they arrived tonight and Scooter had broken the alarm code in a matter of seconds, unlocking the door as if they were being invited right in by an invisible host.

And now…

Now he was discovering that Scooter was equally adept with firearms.

Like the Smith & Wesson .48 special he suddenly pulled.

"But I *am* here. And I'm not letting you destroy my livelihood," the old man said now, despite the gun in Scooter's hand.

Craig was pretty sure that the octogenarian's name had to be Hudson. The sign on the small shop in the valley advertised it as Hudson & Son, Fine Art, Antiques, Memorabilia and Jewelry.

It was the jewelry and antiques they'd come for. Scooter and Quintin were becoming infamous all through the Northeast for knocking off a long string of jewelry and antique stores. They went for family establishments—the type not found in malls. The kind in small towns, where the biggest crimes tended to be speeding or graffiti. They struck, then disappeared, and the insurance agencies were the ones to pay. Easy in, easy out, and no one got hurt, except in the wallet.

Craig had never heard of Scooter or Quintin using a gun.

Then again, he'd never heard of them ripping off a place where someone had remained behind after hours.

But there was a first time for everything. Here, in a little hick town in Massachusetts, they had found the place where someone was still around.

Craig felt ill.

He knew the pair were successful because of Scooter's talent with electronics, which ensured that they were never caught on videotape. No witness could ever describe their faces, because there never were any witnesses. In short, they had never been seen.

Until now.

"Scooter, it's Christmas. Let's just get the hell out of here," Craig said.

Scooter looked at him, shaking his head as he scooped up jewelry and threw it into a bag. "No, sorry, I don't think so. Even if I wanted to, and I don't, I don't think Quintin's ready to go."

That was all too obvious, Craig thought, looking over at the other man. Already Craig had figured out

THE LAST NOEL   11

that, while Scooter talked as if he called the shots, it was Quintin who really ran the operation. And Quintin wasn't all that fond of Craig, so he knew he had to be careful.

"There's got to be a safe, so open it, pops," Quintin was saying now.

"Sir, please," Craig said politely to Mr. Hudson, silently begging the old man to back down and do as he was told. "Open the safe."

"No."

"I'll shoot you, you old fart, and don't think I won't," Scooter told him.

"Do it," the old man said.

"Come on, guys. There's a storm coming in, and we need to get the hell out of here before it does," Craig said. "Why don't we just leave the old guy alone and get out of here?"

"Told you that the kid was a mistake," Quintin said disgustedly to Scooter. Quintin was a big man, but not fat. He was pure muscle, with small dark eyes, a bald head and the shoulders of an orangutan. He was oddly fanatic in his dress. He liked to be neat, and he was fond of designer clothing. He was in his forties, and despite his occupation, he was quite capable of speaking and appearing like a gentleman.

Scooter was just the opposite: thin as a rail. He had a wiry strength, though. Sandy hair worn a little too long, and eyes that were so pale a blue they were almost colorless. Scooter was somewhere in his midthirties, and Craig was becoming more and more convinced that he had some kind of learning disability. He often sounded totally vicious, but at other times his voice held the awe of a child, and he was sometimes slow.

Craig was the youngest of their trio and the newcomer. He wondered just how odd he looked, joined up with the two of them. At twenty-five, he considered himself in good shape, but, of course, the life he'd chosen demanded that he be fit. Bitterness at the past had made him work hard. He was blue-eyed and blond, like the boy next door. Quintin had liked that about him. What Quintin didn't like about him, Craig had never quite figured out.

As they all stood there, at something of an impasse, the store was suddenly cast into pitch-darkness as a loud crack announced the splitting of a nearby power pole.

"Nobody move," Scooter snapped.

A backup generator kicked in almost immediately, and they were bathed in a soft, slightly reddish light. In those few seconds, though, the old man had tried to hit the alarm. Craig could read the truth in his eyes and in the nervous energy that made him shake just slightly. Scooter saw it, too.

"You stupid old fool," Scooter said softly.

"The power was out," Craig said quickly. "The alarm was dead."

"I don't give a damn," Scooter said. "Open the safe. Now!"

But old man Hudson seemed totally indifferent to his own impending doom. He even smiled. "I don't care if you shoot me."

"Just open the safe, sir. What can possibly be in there that's worth your life?" Craig asked.

Quintin looked at him contemptuously.

"Look, you old fool," Quintin said to Hudson, "He won't just shoot you, he'll make you hurt. He'll shoot your kneecaps, and then he'll shoot your teeny-weeny little pecker. Now open the safe!"

"You must have insurance," Craig pointed out reasonably. He was stunned at Quintin's viciousness. Not that he knew the man well. This was actually his first real job with Scooter and Quintin. Before, he had been trying to pass muster. When he'd been taken along tonight, he'd thought he'd been cleared. And he had been—by Scooter. But Quintin was hard.

And Quintin didn't like him. Didn't trust him.

Craig knew they'd worked with another guy before, who hadn't been arrested, and hadn't been found dead. He had just disappeared. And that was how Craig had gotten in.

Well, he'd wanted in, and he'd gotten what he wanted, Craig thought, and swore silently to himself. This wasn't the way it should have gone. And now he was going to have to do something about that.

Scooter still looked ready to shoot. The situation was rapidly turning violent.

Craig reached nonchalantly behind his back for the Glock he carried tucked into his waistband. Before he could produce it, Quintin slammed him on the shoulder. "You've got no bullets, buddy," he said softly.

Craig frowned fiercely, staring at him.

Quintin stared back, dark eyes cool and assessing. "Were you planning to shoot the old man—or one of us?" he asked. "I took away your bullets, *friend*."

"Why'd you do that?" Scooter demanded.

"Didn't you hear me? I don't trust him not to shoot one of us," Quintin said, then turned back to Hudson. "Come on, asshole. It's now or never."

"*You're* the asshole, Quintin," Craig said. Damn it, he thought. What was he going to do without any bullets?

Finally the old man turned and started turning the dial on the safe. As soon as it opened, he stepped away, staring off into the distance, as if none of it meant anything to him anymore.

Craig felt a sudden deep, overwhelming surge of sadness. What the hell was this old man doing alone on Christmas Eve? Where was the son listed on the sign? Where was the rest of his family?

Was this really the sum of life? Men wanted sons. Sons wanted the keys to the car. *Sure, Dad,* the son said. *I'll help with the business.* And then he found something else that interested him more and was gone, until one day Dad was old. And alone.

"Bag it up," Scooter demanded, pointing to the bills and jewelry in the safe. "Bag it all up."

"You know you're not going anywhere, right?" the old man asked calmly.

"Wrong, pops. We're going straight to New York City. Hiding in plain sight," Scooter said happily.

Craig felt his stomach drop. Scooter had just told the old man their plans, not to mention that Hudson had seen their faces. Craig could practically see the death warrant in his mind.

"A nor'easter is coming in," the old man said, sounding so casual. "Hasn't been one this bad in years, I can tell you."

The weather *was* turning; Craig could feel it. The storm that should have gone north of them had veered south instead, he thought, then went back to wondering why Hudson was at work and alone on Christmas Eve.

"Right. Like I'm afraid of a little snow." Scooter sniffed.

Did the old man have a cell phone? Craig wondered. He had lied before. He was certain the man had hit his alarm already, but there were no sirens drawing near, no sign of help.

Now, with no indication of panic or hurry, the man started filling the bag Scooter handed him with bills and jewelry.

"We got it all. Let's go," Craig said.

"*You* go," Quintin said. "Get in the driver's seat and wait for us. And don't fuck up."

"Let's all get the hell out of here," Craig said. "Come on. You've got what you came for."

"Wuss." Quintin sniffed. "Or worse."

"What do you mean, worse?" Scooter asked.

"Cop."

"I'm no cop. I just don't want to do life over a couple of lousy bracelets," Craig said, but he felt a bead of sweat on his upper lip. Quintin was one scary SOB. His eyes were like glass. No emotion, empathy or remorse lay anywhere behind that stare.

"The old guy's seen our faces, and thanks to

Scooter—" he shot the man a scathing glance "—he knows where we're going," Quintin said.

"And he's probably legally blind and totally deaf," Craig argued.

"I'm not taking that chance," Quintin said harshly.

"And I'm not going to be party to murder," Craig said and turned to appeal to the other man. "Scooter, you're an idiot if you listen to this thug," he said. "We'll all get locked away forever for murder, and I'm not as old as you guys. I don't want to spend the next fifty years without a woman."

Quintin started to laugh. "Don't worry about it, kid. They lock up people like Martha Stewart. Killers, hell, they get to walk away free. Crazy, isn't it?"

"Craig...we gotta do what Quintin says," Scooter insisted.

"Even if what he says is stupid?" Craig asked.

"Fuck you," Quintin said, casually pulling out a gun. "Keep talking like that and you won't have to worry about jail."

Craig assessed his situation. No question it was dire. He was probably in the best shape of his life, and he was the youngest of the three of them. In a fair fight, he could probably take out Quintin, no matter that the man was an ape. But there were two of them. And it wasn't going to be a fair fight. Because they had guns. With bullets.

There would never be a fair fight with Quintin.

He turned to plead with Scooter again, but he was too late. Quintin, moving faster than Craig would have thought possible for a man his size, cracked Craig on the head with the butt of his gun.

Craig literally saw stars, and then the world went black.

As he sank to the ground, he heard the deafening sound of an explosion.

The blast of a gun…

He'd screwed up.

What a great, last thought to have—and on Christmas Eve.

As he sank into unconsciousness, he was certain he could hear the familiar refrain of a Christmas carol.

Oh, tidings of comfort and joy.

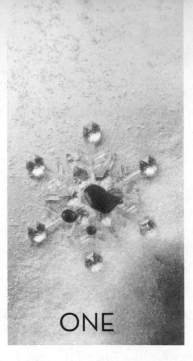

ONE

The stereo was on, playing songs of Christmas cheer. Skyler O'Boyle took a moment to listen to a woman with a high, clear voice who was singing, "Sleigh bells ring, are you lis'nin'…"

Then, even over the music and from her place in the kitchen, she heard the yelling.

"I said hold it. Hold the tree!"

Skyler winced.

Christmas. Home for the holidays, merry, merry, ho, ho, ho, family love, world peace.

In her family? Yeah, right.

The expected answer came, and the voice was just as loud. "I *am* holding it," her eldest son insisted.

"Straight, dammit, Frazier. Hold it straight," her husband, David, snapped irritably.

In her mind's eye, Skyler could see them, David on the floor, trying to wedge the tree into the stand, and Frazier, standing, trying to hold the tree straight. That was what happened when you decided "home for the holidays" meant everyone gathering in the old family house out in the country. It meant throwing everything together at the last possible moment, because everyone had to juggle their school and work schedules with their holiday vacation.

"The frigging needles are poking my eyes. This is the best I can do," Frazier complained in what sounded suspiciously like a growl.

His tone was sure to aggravate his father, she thought.

Some people got Christmas cheer; she got David and Frazier fighting over the tree.

Where the hell had the spirit of the season gone, at least in her family? Actually, if she wanted to get philosophical, where had the spirit of the season gone in a large part of the known world? There were no real Norman Rockwell paintings. People walked by the Salvation Army volunteers without a glance; it seemed as if the only reason anyone put money in the kettle was that they were burdened by so much change that it was actually too heavy for comfort. Then they beat each other up over the latest electronic toy to hit the market.

"It's nowhere near straight," David roared.

"Put up your own fucking tree, then," Frazier shouted.

"Son of a bitch…" David swore.

"…*walkin' in a winter wonderland.*"

Please, God, Skyler prayed silently, *don't let my husband and my son come to blows on Christmas Eve.*

"Hey, Kat, you there?"

Great, Skyler thought. Now David was getting their daughter involved.

"Yeah, Dad, I'm here. But I can't hold that tree any straighter. And I hope Brenda didn't hear you two yelling," Kat said.

Skyler headed out toward the living room, ready

to head off a major family disaster, and paused just out of sight in the hall.

Had she been wrong? Should she have told her son he shouldn't bring Brenda home for the holidays? He'd turned twenty-two. He could have told her that he wasn't coming home, in that case, and was going to spend the holidays with Brenda's family. And then she would have been without her firstborn child. Of course, that was going to happen somewhere along the line anyway; that was life. With the kids getting older, it was already hard to get the entire family together.

"Oh, so now I have to worry—in my own house—about offending the girl who came here to sleep with my son?" David complained.

David wasn't a bad man, Skyler thought. He wasn't even a bad father. But he had different ideas about what was proper and what wasn't. They had been children themselves, really, when they had gotten married. She had been eighteen, and he had been nineteen. But even as desperately in love as they had been, there was no way either of them could have told their parents that they were going to live together.

Current mores might be much wiser, she reflected. Most of *her* generation seemed to be divorced.

"What century are you living in, Dad?" Frazier demanded. Apparently his train of thought was running alongside hers. "There's nothing wrong with Brenda staying in my room. It's not as if we don't sleep together back at school. You should trust my judgment. And don't go getting all 'I'm so respectable, this girl better be golden.' We're not exactly royalty, Dad. We own a bar," he finished dryly.

"We own a pub, a fine family place," David snapped back irritably. "And what's that supposed to mean, anyway? That pub is paying for college for both you and your sister."

"I'm just saying that some people wouldn't consider owning a bar the height of morality."

"Morality?" David exploded. "We've never once been cited for underage drinking, and we're known across the country for bringing the best in Celtic music to the States."

"Dad, it's all right," Kat said soothingly. "And you…shut the hell up," she said, and elbowed her brother in the ribs. "Both of you—play nice."

Skyler held her breath as Frazier walked away and headed upstairs, probably to make sure his girlfriend hadn't heard her name evoked in the family fight.

It was probably best. Her husband and son were always at each other's throats, it seemed, while Kat was the family peacemaker, who could ease the toughest situation. She'd gone through her own period of teenage rebellion on the way to becoming an adult, and getting along with her had been hell for a while. But that was over, and now Kat was like Skyler's miracle of optimism, beautiful and sweet. A dove of peace.

She wanted to think that she was a dove of peace herself, but she wasn't and she knew it.

She was just a chicken. A chicken who hated harsh tones and the sounds of disagreement. Sometimes she was even a lying chicken, for the sake of keeping the peace.

But this was Christmas. She had to say something to David. He really shouldn't be using that tone—not here, not now and not with Frazier.

Frazier just… He just wasn't a child anymore. He didn't always act like an adult, but that didn't make him a child. David was far too quick to judge and to judge harshly, while she was too quick to let anything go, all for the sake of peace. There had been hundreds of times through the years when she should have stepped in, put her foot down. She'd failed. So how could she blame others now for doing what she'd always allowed them to do?

At last she stepped out of the shadows of the hallway and looked at the tree. "It's lovely," she said.

"It's crooked," David told her, his mouth set in a hard line.

"It's fine," she insisted softly.

"That's what I say, Mom," Kat said. She was twenty-two, as well, their second-born child and Frazier's twin. She walked over to Skyler and set an arm around her mother's shoulders. "I'll get going on the lights."

"*I'll* get the lights up," David said. "You can take it from there."

Skyler looked at her daughter. Kat could still show her temper on occasion, but she could stand against her father with less friction than Frazier. Maybe the problem with David and Frazier was a testosterone thing, like in a pride of lions. There was only room for one alpha male.

But this was Christmas. Couldn't they all get along? At least on Christmas Eve and Christmas Day? Other people counted their blessings; shouldn't they do the same? They had three beautiful, healthy children: Jamie, their youngest son, was sixteen, and then there were the twins. None of them had ever been in serious trouble—just that one prank of Jamie's, and that should be enough for anyone, shouldn't it?

"Mom," Kat said, "I'll decorate. Anyone who wants to can just pitch in."

David was already struggling with the lights, but he paused to look at Skyler for a moment. He still had the powerful look of a young man. His hair was thick and dark, with just a few strands of what she privately felt were a very *dignified* gray. She had been the one to pass on the rich red hair to her children, but the emerald-gold eyes that were so bewitching on Kat had come from her father.

Where have the years gone? she wondered, looking at him. He was still a good-looking and interesting man, but it was easy to forget that sometimes. And sometimes it was easy to wonder if being married wasn't more a habit than a commitment of the heart.

Skyler winced. She loved her family. Desperately. Too desperately?

David cursed beneath his breath, then exploded. "They can put a man on the moon, but they can't invent Christmas lights that don't tangle and make you check every freaking bulb."

"Dad, they do make lights where the whole string doesn't go if one bulb is blown. Our lights are just old," Kat explained patiently.

Skyler looked at her daughter, feeling a rush of emotion that threatened to become tears. She loved her children equally, but at this moment Kat seemed exceptionally precious. She was stunning, of course, with her long auburn hair. Tall and slim—though, like many young women, she was convinced she needed to take off ten pounds. Those eyes like gold-flecked emeralds. And she had an amazing head on her shoulders.

"Yeah, well…if we stayed in Boston and *prepared* for Christmas…" David muttered.

Not fair, she thought. He was the one who had found this place years ago and he'd fallen in love with it first. Once upon a time, they had come here often. The kids had loved to leave the city and drive the two hours out to the country. They never left the state, but they went from the sea to the mountains. And everyone loved it.

She realized why she had wanted to come here so badly. It was a way to keep her family around her. It was a way to make sure that if her son and his father got into a fight over the Christmas turkey, Frazier couldn't just get up and drive off to a friend's house. Was it wrong to cling so desperately to her children and her dream of family?

"Mom, need any help in the kitchen?" Kat asked. It was clearly going to be a while until the lights were up and she could start on the ornaments.

Skyler shook her head. "Actually, I'm fine. Everything is more or less ready. We're going traditional Irish tonight—corned beef, bacon, cabbage and potatoes, and it's all in one pot. We can eat soon. Tomorrow we'll have turkey."

"Want me to set the table while Dad argues with the lights?" Kat asked.

Skyler grinned. "See if you can help him argue with the lights, and I'll set the table. We'll just eat in the kitchen, where it's warm and cozy."

Kat smiled at her mother.

Skyler couldn't have asked for a better daughter, she thought as she made her way back to the kitchen. They shared clothes and confidences, and she had learned not to worry every time her daughter drove away.

With her daughter here…

Skyler felt as if there were a chance for a Norman Rockwell Christmas after all.

Frazier came running down the stairs, followed by Brenda. They were an attractive couple, she had to admit. He was so tall, muscled without being bulky, with hair a deeper shade of red than his sister's. And he, too, had his father's eyes. Next to him, Brenda was tiny, delicate. And blond.

"Way too perfect," Kat had told her mother teasingly, since she'd met Brenda first.

"You might want to turn on the TV and check the weather update," Frazier said.

"That storm is getting worse," Brenda added shyly.

"Really?" Skyler said, offering Brenda what she

hoped was a welcoming smile. Not only was Brenda tiny and blond, her brilliant blue eyes made her look like a true little snow princess. Skyler had been relieved to learn that she was twenty-one. When she'd first met the young woman, she'd been terrified that Frazier had fallen for a teenager, but Brenda simply looked young because she was so petite. She tended to be shy, but she certainly seemed very sweet.

Okay, it would be nice if she talked a bit more to someone in the house other than Frazier, but really, what wasn't to like about her?

David was too entangled in the lights to find the remote. Skyler saw it on a chair and flicked the TV on. A serious-looking anchorman was delivering a warning.

"We're looking at major power outages, and despite the fact that it's Christmas Eve, because the weather is already turning vicious, we suggest that anyone who may have medical or other difficulties in the event of a power loss get to a hospital or a shelter now. And everyone should be prepared, with candles and flashlights within reach."

"Ah-ha!" David cried, and they all turned to stare at him.

He shrugged weakly. "Sorry. I untangled the lights."

"Let's get 'em up, and then let's eat," Skyler suggested cheerfully. "With luck we can finish before the power blows, and if it does, we can play Scrabble by candlelight or something."

"Wretched weather," Kat muttered, her attention turning back to the television. "Mom, Dad, why didn't we buy a house on a Caribbean island?"

"We couldn't afford a house on a Caribbean island," David said, but he sounded a lot more cheerful than he had earlier. He hesitated, then said, "Frazier, will you grab that end?"

Frazier hesitated, as well, before saying, "Sure, Dad."

"Good. You two deal with the lights, and I'll get the food on the table," Skyler said.

"Let's get Mister Sixteen and Rebellious down here, too, huh?" Kat said. "He can give us a hand."

"Good idea, and would you get Uncle Paddy, too?"

There was a short silence after she spoke. Perhaps she'd even imagined it, she thought.

David wasn't thrilled about her uncle being there,

she knew, and she was suddenly thankful that they'd both been born the children of Irish immigrants. He would never expect her to actually turn away a relative, even if he felt that Paddy was a drunk who deserved whatever he was suffering now. Which wasn't really fair, she thought, but David was entitled to his opinion.

Often enough, Uncle Paddy was the real Irish entertainment at the pub. In his own way, of course.

Kat sprang to life, dispelling whatever awkwardness there might have been. She grinned and ran halfway up the stairs, then called, "Jamie! Jamie O'Boyle! Get your delinquent ass down here on the double. Uncle Paddy…dinner."

"I could have yelled myself," Skyler said.

"But you'd never have used such poetic language," Kat said, and even David laughed.

The first thing Craig realized when he came to was that his head was killing him.

Quintin packed one hell of a wallop.

He didn't know how long he'd been out, didn't know how far they had come. All he knew was that even from where he lay, tossed into the backseat of their stolen vehicle, when he first cracked his eyes open it looked like the whole world had turned white.

Impossible.

He closed his eyes again, waited a long moment, then reopened them. The world was still white. It was snow, and not just snow, but fiercely blowing snow. Hell. It was a nor'easter and a mean one. A blizzard.

He ached all over and wondered if anything in his body was broken.

And what about the old man they had robbed?

His stomach tightened painfully when he caught sight of a familiar stand of trees and realized he knew exactly where they were. For a moment, memories filled his mind and drove away the pain, and then every muscle in his body tensed in an effort at self-preservation, as the car suddenly spun and came to a violent halt in a snowdrift.

"Asshole!" Quintin shouted from the front seat.

"You're the asshole," Scooter returned savagely. "You try driving in this shit."

"Doesn't matter now. We're stuck. We'll have to get out and walk."

"We're in the middle of nowhere!" Scooter protested.

"No, we're not. There's a house right up there," Quintin snapped, pointing. "I can see the lights in the windows."

"What? We're going to drop in for Christmas dinner?" Scooter demanded angrily.

"It's still Christmas Eve," Quintin said. "The season of peace and goodwill toward men."

"Fine. We're going to crash somebody's Christmas *Eve* dinner?" Scooter asked, sounding doubtful, even disbelieving, and thoroughly uneasy.

"That's exactly what we're going to do," Quintin said.

Craig's head was still in agony. Despite that, he felt a terrible sense of dread. Inwardly, he cringed, his mind screaming.

He knew that house. He had dropped by often in a different time.

In a different life.

He remembered it so well: set on a little hill, a beautiful house, comfortable and warm, a place where a family—a real family—gathered and cooked and celebrated the holidays.

How could they have settled on that house? How could the fates be that unfair? It wasn't even right on the road, for God's sake; they should never even have known it was there as they drove past in the storm.

"We've got to get away from here. Far away," Scooter argued.

Good thought, Craig approved silently.

"Far away?" Quintin mocked. "You're out of your mind. Just how far do you think we can get in this weather, without a car—seeing as someone drove ours into a snowdrift? We need a place to stay. Are you insane? Can't you see? We're not going to get anywhere tonight."

Scooter was silent for a moment, then said, "We shouldn't see people tonight."

"Don't you mean people shouldn't see us?" Quintin asked. He laughed. "Like it will make a difference. Whatever we have to do, we'll do."

In the back, eyes shut again as he pretended he was still unconscious, Craig shuddered inwardly and considered his options. Depending on how he looked at things, they went from few to nonexistent.

Sorrow ripped through him at the thought of the

old man they had left behind, followed by a fresh onslaught of dread.

He prayed in silence, trying desperately to think of
a way out and cursing fate for his present situation.

How the hell had he ended up here? And tonight
of all nights?

"Ah, me poor bones," Uncle Paddy moaned when
Kat went up to repeat the news that dinner was
ready, although he looked quite comfortable, reclin-
ing against a stack of pillows on the very nice daybed
that sat near the radiator in the guest room. He had
been happily watching television, and he'd apparently gotten her mother to bring him up some tea
and cookies earlier. She suspected he hadn't been in
a speck of pain until she'd knocked briefly and
opened the door to his room.

She stared at him, then set her hands on her hips
and slipped into an echo of his accent. "Your old
bones are just fine, Uncle Patrick. It's no sympathy
you'll be getting tonight."

Her uncle looked at her indignantly—a look he'd
mastered, she thought.

"A few drops of whiskey would be makin' 'em a whole lot better, me fine lass."

"Maybe later."

"I've got to be getting down the stairs," he said.

"Uncle Paddy, even I know it's easier to get down a flight of stairs *before* taking a shot of whiskey," Jamie said from behind Kat, making her start in surprise. So her little brother had finally left the haven of his room, she thought. He was only sixteen, but already a good three inches taller than she was. He even had an inch on Frazier these days. He was thin, with a lean, intelligent face. He worried that he didn't look tough enough, but he wasn't exactly planning to be a boxer. He was a musician, something that came easily enough in their family. He loved his guitar, and when he played a violin, grown men had been known to weep.

It occurred to her that she hadn't spent a lot of time with him in the last year, and this was a time in his life when he could use some sane guidance from his older siblings. She remembered being sixteen all too well.

The opposite sex. Peer pressure. Drugs. Cigarettes.

Once, she'd thought of him almost as her own baby. Even though there were only six years between them, she'd been old enough to help out when he'd been born. Then again, they hadn't grown up in the usual household. Their home was by Boston Common, the pub closer to the wharf, and they'd all spent plenty of time in that pub. When she'd been a teenager, her friends had enjoyed the mistaken belief that she could supply liquor for whatever party they were planning.

She could still remember the pressure, and the pain of finding out that some of her so-called friends lost all interest in her when she wouldn't go along with their illegal plans. It wasn't until she'd had her heart seriously broken her first year of college that she'd learned to depend on herself for her own happiness. That she could be depressed and work in her parents' pub all her life or she could create her own dreams.

Age and experience. She had both, she decided, at the grand age of twenty-two.

She smiled at how self-righteous she sounded in her own mind. Well, maybe she was, but she knew she was never going to make the mistakes her parents had made. She wasn't going to live her life entirely for others. Oh, she meant to have children. And it looked as if Uncle Paddy was around to stay. But she was never going to torture herself over her husband's temper or the bickering that went on around her.

To hell with them all; that would be her motto. God could sort them out later.

But, for the moment, she realized, she was concerned about Jamie—and the fact he had been so quick to lock himself away. What had he been up to?

She knew, despite her mother's determination to keep certain situations private between herself and a particular child, that Jamie had gotten himself into some minor trouble up here last year. Luckily for him, a sheriff's deputy had just come to the house and commented on how easily calls could be traced these days.

"You're behaving, right?" she said to him now.

He'd been in his room since they'd gotten there. Of course, he'd made no secret of the fact that he thought she and Frazier should deal with their father on holidays, seeing as the two of them got to escape back to college after a few days, while he had to deal with his parents on a daily basis.

Jamie just grinned and nodded toward Uncle Paddy, who had taken offense at Jamie's last comment and was staring at his youngest nephew with his head held high in indignation.

"At my age, a bit of whiskey is medicinal," he announced.

"Yeah, whatever," Jamie said irreverently. "But the whiskey is downstairs. So grab your cane, and we'll be your escort."

Kat grinned. Maybe this Christmas would be okay after all, despite its somewhat rocky start.

"Come on, Uncle Paddy. You're not that old, so move it," Jamie said.

"There is simply no respect for seniors in this house," Paddy said. "The abuse your poor wee mother takes…" He shook his head.

"My mother is neither poor nor wee," Kat retorted. "Now come on. It's Christmas, and we're going to have fun and be happy."

"Yes, dammit. Whether we like it or not," Jamie agreed.

Kat reached for Paddy's arm. With a groan, he rose. "Ah, me old bones."

"Your old palate can have a wee dram the minute we get you down the stairs," Jamie assured him.

Paddy arched a brow. "Are ye joinin' me then, lad?"

"Sure, it's Christmas."

"Ye're not of an age."

"Like you were?" Jamie said, rolling his eyes.

"This is America."

"So?" Jamie said. "My parents run a bar. It's not like I haven't had a shot now and then."

Paddy let out an oath. Kat knew what it was because she'd been told as a child never to learn Gaelic from Uncle Paddy. Luckily, not many people spoke Gaelic, so they seldom knew what he was saying when he was out and about and swearing at the world.

Now he waved a hand at them and headed for the stairs under his own power. "The young. No respect," he muttered, then raised his cane and shook it at them.

They both laughed and followed him downstairs.

Skyler had all but the last of the food on the table when Uncle Paddy entered the kitchen and headed straight for the liquor cabinet.

"Your beer's on the table," she said, her tone slightly sharp. She realized that she was looking over her shoulder, hoping that David hadn't seen Paddy heading straight for the whiskey.

"I'll take a beer, too," Jamie said cheerfully, coming in behind Paddy.

"Jamie…" she said warningly.

"It's better than the hard stuff, right?" Jamie asked.

"Actually, I think a beer and a shot have about the same alcohol content," Kat said, following her brother into the kitchen.

"What, now our son is heading straight for the liquor, too?" David demanded harshly from behind Kat.

His words tightened the knot of tension already forming between Skyler's shoulder blades as she remembered the "incident" with Jamie.

"Jeez, Dad, would you lighten up?" Jamie demanded.

"Great. I knew we should have gone to your family," Frazier murmured to Brenda, as they walked into the middle of the argument.

Take control, Skyler told herself angrily. All your

life, you let things go, trying to maintain the peace. Now for once in your life, do something. "David, Jamie, please," she said. "It's Christmas Eve."

"We own a bar," Jamie said. "What's the big deal?"

"Stop it, Jamie. Stop it now," she said firmly, wondering why family gatherings had to be such a nightmare.

"Pub," David corrected irritably. "And that's no reason for my kids to be drunks, too."

"Ye'd be referring to me, eh?" Paddy demanded.

Take control, Skyler ordered herself. And finally spoke up. "Uncle Paddy, you have a drinking problem, and you know it. Jamie, you may have a beer. One." She stared at her husband. "I'd rather he drink with us than away from us, if he's going to drink. And he *is* going to drink. So...sit down. Kat, Frazier, Brenda, what would *you* like to drink?"

"Just water for me," Brenda said hurriedly.

Of course someone so slim and tiny wouldn't consume a liquid with calories, Skyler thought. Then again, at least the girl had answered on her own. She had been so quiet since her arrival.

She was shy. Not like this group.

"Frazier, what will you have?"

"I'll have a beer—if Dad doesn't think it will turn me into an alcoholic."

David stared at his older son, still irritated.

"Don't be silly. Your father knows that you don't abuse alcohol."

"Yeah. Not like some of those old boozehounds at the pub," Frazier said.

"Boozehounds? Those fine fellows put food on your plate," Paddy said.

"Including the ones who fall off their bar stools?" Frazier asked.

"We don't serve drunks," David snapped.

"Dad's right," Kat said, grinning, "We reserve the right not to serve people who are falling off the bar stools."

"Even when they're our relatives," Jamie chimed in.

"Jamie…" Skyler cautioned with a sigh. So much for taking control. David was clearly taking every word seriously, which did not bode well for a pleasant meal.

"Mom, what would *you* like to drink?" Kat asked.

Skyler hesitated, shaking her head. "Hell. Just give me the whole bottle of whiskey."

To her amazement, there was silence.

Then laughter.

Even David's lips twitched.

"Come on, guys, let's all behave," Kat said. "We're driving Mom to drink."

"Let's eat," Skyler said with forced cheer. "Sit down already."

"You want us anywhere in particular?" Kat asked, walking up behind her mother and hugging her.

"In a chair at the table, that's all," she said, and gave her daughter a little squeeze in return.

"We're short a place setting," Kat noted.

"No, we're not."

"Yes, we are. Count," Kat said.

"There are six place settings, and five of us and…Brenda and Paddy," Skyler said. "I'm sorry. I'll get another plate."

"I'll go find a chair," Kat said. "I think there's an extra in the den."

"I'm so sorry, guys," Skyler said as Kat hurried out.

"That's okay, Mom. You can't count, but we love you anyway," Frazier teased, smiling at her.

She smiled back. "And Dad?"

His smiled wavered for a moment. "We love Dad, too, of course. Although I think he can count."

"Cute," Skyler said. "Brenda, please sit down and just ignore my family."

Uncle Paddy was staring at her questioningly, and Brenda looked acutely uncomfortable. How the hell had she miscounted? She just hadn't been thinking clearly. She'd been too busy listening in on other people's conversations. Worrying.

She didn't want arguing. She wanted peace and the whole Norman Rockwell picture.

"I'm sorry for intruding on your family Christmas—" Brenda began.

"Don't be silly, you're not intruding in the least, and we're delighted to have you. I'm just getting absentminded in my old age," Skyler said.

"It's all those years in a bar," Frazier teased.

"Pub," David said.

"Beer fumes," Jamie put in.

David groaned exaggeratedly. "All right, enough with the pub and the beer. Brenda, you are entirely welcome here. Please sit down."

"Please," Skyler echoed. "Jamie likes to say that I

have adult attention deficiency disorder. Personally, I think it comes from my children," she explained, staring firmly from one of her sons to the other. "Let's all sit and enjoy our dinner."

Suddenly the doorbell rang.

Skyler looked at her husband, who looked back at her, his eyebrows arching questioningly. "You have more company coming?" he asked. His tone, at least, was light. "Someone's long-lost relative? Stray friend?"

She glared at him fiercely. "No."

"Why would anyone be traveling in this weather?" Brenda mused.

So she did speak without being spoken to, Skyler thought, then wanted to kick herself for the unkind thought. But the girl was so quiet most of the time. Probably, her family didn't fight all the time, and she just felt uncomfortable, intimidated.

"Someone might have had an accident, Dad," Frazier suggested.

"If someone is hurt or stranded, of course they can come in," Skyler said quickly.

"What idiot would be out in this weather?" David asked.

The bell sounded again.

"We could just answer the blasted thing and find out what's going on," Paddy said.

"I'll get it," Jamie said.

"No. I'll get it," David said firmly. "You all just sit."

But no one sat.

David led, Skyler close behind him, everyone else behind her. The swinging door that separated the kitchen from the dining room, which sat to the one side of the entry, thumped as one person after another pushed it on the way through.

The bell rang again.

"Hurry, someone might be freezing out there," Skyler said.

And yet, even as she spoke, she felt a strange sense of unease.

Somehow Norman Rockwell seemed to be slipping away.

And she—who took in any stray puppy, who always helped the down and out, animal or human— didn't want David to open the door.

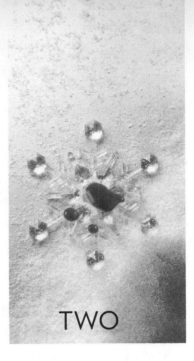

TWO

The chair in the den lost a leg the minute Kat picked it up. She let out a groan of frustration and tried to put it back on.

It would go back on, but it wouldn't stay, because a crucial screw seemed to be missing. She looked around, getting down on hands and knees to see if it had rolled into a corner somewhere. No luck.

No problem. There was a chair at the desk up in her room, and she knew it was fine, because she had been sitting in it earlier while she was online.

She was upstairs when she heard the doorbell

ring. Curious, she walked to the window and looked out. She saw a car stuck nose-first in a snowdrift, barely off the road, down where the slope of their yard began.

The bell rang again, and two men backed out from beneath the porch roof and stared up at the house. Strangers. She could barely see them; the wind was really blowing the snow around, and they were bundled up in coats, scarves and hats, but something about their movement made her think that they were in their thirties—late twenties to forty, tops, at any rate.

She frowned, watching as they moved back out of sight and the bell rang for a third time.

Not at all sure why, she didn't grab the chair and run down the stairs. Instead, she found herself walking quietly out to the landing, where she stood in the shadows, looking and listening.

"We know it's Christmas Eve," one man was saying.

"And we're so sorry," said the second.

"But we ran off the road and we need help," said the first.

"A dog shouldn't be out on a night like this," said the second.

"We were just about to sit down to dinner." Her father's voice, and he sounded suspicious. Good.

"Dinner," the first man repeated.

Peering carefully over the banister, still strangely unwilling to give herself away, Kat tried to get a look at the men. One was bulky and well-dressed, and shorter than her father and Frazier by a few inches; since they were about six-one to Jamie's six-two, that made the stranger about six feet even.

The other man, the one who had spoken first, was leaner. He had the look of…a sidekick? Odd thought, but that was exactly the word that occurred to her. He needed a haircut, and his coat was missing several buttons. Even his knit cap looked as if it had seen better days.

When the heavier man took off his hat, he was bald—clean-shaven bald. He had thick dark brows, and eyes that were set too close together.

Beady eyes, Kat thought, then chided herself for watching too much *C.S.I.*

"Good heavens, come in and get out of the cold," her mother told the pair.

Her mother would have taken in Genghis Khan,

Kat thought, although she didn't sound entirely happy about extra guests at the moment. Maybe because it was Christmas Eve, she decided. But really, what choice was there? The two men could hardly go anywhere else.

But what the hell were they doing out to begin with? Maybe they didn't live here near the mountains, but anyone who lived anywhere in New England knew how treacherous the weather could become in a matter of hours, and the TV and radio stations had been talking nonstop about this storm for two days before it even got here. It had been touch and go whether the family even made it up here in time.

"Thank you, ma'am, and bless you," the tall man said, holding out his hand. "I'm William Blane, but folks call me Scooter. And this is my associate, Mr. Quintin Lark."

"How do you do, and I, too, thank you," the stocky man said.

Her father looked at her mother and smiled in solidarity. At that moment, despite the bickering that never seemed to stop, she was reminded of how much she loved her parents. And that she was proud of them. Her father worked hard, doing everything around the pub. He lugged boxes and kept the books, but he could pick up a fiddle or a keyboard and sit in with a band, and he was always willing to pitch in and wash glasses. He managed the kitchen, the bar and the inventory.

And her mother... Her mother had raised three children, working all the while. Like Kat's dad, her mom could sit in with the band. She had a clear soprano and a gift for the piano. She served drinks and meals, tended bar and always picked up a broom and a dust rag when needed.

Her mother was the key element that truly turned the place from a bar into a pub, Kat decided. She *listened*. She knew their customers. She knew that Mrs. O'Malley's cat had produced five kittens and that those kittens were as important to Mrs. O'Malley as Mr. Browne's new grandson was to him. She knew old man Adair had gotten part of a mortar shell in his calf during the war—World War II, that was— and that as stubborn and sturdy as the old fellow might appear, his leg ached on an hourly basis. Her mother cared about people, perhaps too much. And in her pursuit of constant cheer, she had often sacrificed the truth.

Even now, she was frowning sympathetically. "You say you had an accident? Where? What happened?"

"We didn't listen to the weather report, I'm afraid," Quintin said.

"We were listening to a CD, instead of the news," Scooter said. "We ran off the road just at the edge of your property. I wasn't even sure we'd make it this far."

"Not to worry," Skyler said. "We have plenty of food. Come on into the kitchen."

"I'll just get some more chairs," David said.

"Wasn't—" Jamie began.

"No," Skyler said firmly, staring at Jamie. "No…we'll be fine in the kitchen. We just need more chairs."

Kat's jaw dropped. Her mother—her *mother*—was suspicious.

And pretending that she wasn't in the house.

"Right," her father said. "Two more chairs. Jamie, take Quintin and, uh, Scooter into the kitchen. Get them a drink."

"A shot of whiskey," Skyler said. "You both need a good shot of whiskey. Just to warm up." She sounded nervous, Kat thought, though no one who didn't know her would notice.

"Whiskey sounds great," Scooter said.

"Let's all go into the kitchen," Quintin added, and Kat thought she heard something ominous in his voice.

"I've got to get more chairs," David said.

"No," Scooter said softly.

It should have been a perfect holiday tableau: a family opening their doors to stranded travelers on a cold and stormy Christmas Eve.

But something just wasn't right. It was as if the picture was out of focus.

Everyone just stood there awkwardly. And then, subtly, Quintin's face changed.

Kat could see the way he smiled. It was a slow smile. A scary smile.

"We need to stay together. All of us," Quintin told them.

Kat felt as if she were staring down at a scene in a play, and someone had forgotten a line.

What in God's name had tipped everyone off?

How had her mother, the soul of trust, figured out—and so quickly—that there was something unsavory about their uninvited guests?

And how had the creep, Quintin, realized that her parents were suspicious?

"This is my house," David said. "We're happy to keep you from freezing to death, but you'll behave by my rules in my house."

"Can't, sorry," Scooter said. He actually looked a little sad.

"Oh? Come on now, we were just about to have dinner, so let's all honor the spirit of the holiday and sit down together."

Good acting job, Dad, Kat cheered silently, then realized that it hadn't made any difference.

Quintin was staring at her mother. "What made you become so mistrustful? Surely you're not a detective, but…a psychiatrist, perhaps? No matter. Yes, this is your house. But I'm the one with a gun. In fact, my friend Scooter has a gun, too. Neither one of us wants to hurt you, but we're outnumbered. Thankfully, you seem to be a nice family. A smart family. So I'm sure you'll see the wisdom of behaving when I tell you that if any one of you gets out of line… Mom here gets it. So the rest of you might be able to take us, but you'd go through the rest of your neat little suburban lives without a mom. So we all stay together," he said softly. "Can't take any chances. After all, you might have a gun of your own squirreled away somewhere," he said, turning to her father.

"Bullshit!"

Her father was a big man—in good shape, as well. He lunged at Quintin, and her brothers, bless them, followed his lead. But Quintin was fast. He pulled his gun before her father got to him.

"Stop now, or Mom is dead!" Quintin roared.

The sound of a bullet blasting ripped through the night, followed by the shattering of glass exploding into a thousand pieces, as Scooter took out a lamp.

"Nobody move," Quintin said.

Everybody stood still, as ordered. Brenda started to cry.

"Shut up!" Quinton said.

Frazier put his arm around Brenda, drawing her close to him.

Uncle Paddy seemed the least disturbed of all of

them. He seemed to be assessing the invaders with remarkably sober eyes.

"No more heroics," Quintin said. "We've given you one chance. Next time, someone dies. Because I'm not going to prison again, ever. I'd rather die first. And if I'm going to die, I'll happily take someone with me. Understand?"

Her poor father, Kat thought. She had never seen him in so much agony. His whole family was threatened, and he was powerless.

A sense of panic seized Kat, like a wave of cold that washed over her and left her trembling. For a moment the world went black. She fell back against the wall in an effort to remain vertical as she fought the nausea that seemed to grip her stomach with an icy, merciless hand.

She inhaled deeply and tried to think. Despite their threats, she didn't know if the pair had ever actually murdered anyone. They were probably thieves. On the other hand...

They were armed. And they had introduced themselves, she realized with a further wave of nausea. That could only mean that whether they'd killed before or not, they weren't planning to leave any witnesses. She shuddered, fear threatening to consume her. She only hoped they hadn't realized just how much danger they were in.

She fought it. She was the only hope her family had.

"All right, folks, if we're all calm, we can get through this. I want your cell phones. Now," Quintin said.

Jamie and Frazier reached into their pockets. As Jamie handed his over, he said, "There's no service out here now, anyway. We're lucky to stand on the roof and get service even when there isn't a storm."

"You never know. Come on, come on, the rest of the cell phones," Quintin said.

David immediately produced his from his pocket.

"Mine's in my purse," Brenda squeaked.

"And where would that be?"

"Right there—the table by the door," Frazier said.

"Get it," Quintin ordered him.

"How about you, Mom? Where's yours?"

"Don't you call her *Mom,*" Jamie warned.

"Jamie…" David said.

"My name is Skyler," her mother told the men.

"Fine. Skyler, where's your phone?"

"In the kitchen, charging," she said.

"And yours, pops?" Quintin asked Paddy as Frazier handed over Brenda's phone.

"I wouldn't be havin' one of those new-fangled things," Uncle Paddy said.

"Everyone in the entire world has a cell phone," Quintin said.

"I'd not be the entire world," Paddy said.

"Watch it, old man," Quintin warned.

"He really doesn't have a cell phone," Frazier interjected.

Quintin eyed him long and hard. "You're a big kid. Feisty, I imagine, like your dad. Don't go playing Superman. I do mean it. You do, and someone will die."

"He's not going to be Superman," Skyler said quickly. "None of us will, okay?"

"Just remember this. I will not go back to prison," Quintin said.

"Let's eat," Scooter said cheerfully, and actually gave her father a friendly punch on the shoulder. "So how is the missus in the kitchen? Is she a good cook?"

"It's all right, David," Skyler said softly, when he started tensing. She stared at him, her eyes pleading.

David managed to choke out an answer. "She's a wonderful cook. And you obviously mean what you say, so don't worry. We'll cooperate in every way."

"Bastards," Uncle Paddy suddenly hissed, thumping his cane for emphasis.

"Paddy, quit banging your cane and shut up," her mother snapped. "We'll have no one dying here tonight. Jamie and Frazier, Scooter can accompany you to the family room. Just grab the bar stools—I'll be happy to sit on one."

"Me, too," Brenda chimed in, the tear tracks drying on her cheeks.

"Quintin, you can join the rest of us in the kitchen."

Her mother had somehow taken control. Amazing, Kat marveled.

Quintin laughed. "Yes, ma'am. We seem to have ourselves an Irish matriarch here, Scooter. There's no one fiercer. And she's a fine cook, we're told. Good thing, because I'm starving. And freezing."

"There are sweaters in the hall closet, right over there," Skyler said, pointing. "Take off your coats. I don't want you sitting at my table in those filthy coats."

Mom, be careful! They'll shoot you for sure, Kat thought, her heart sinking.

But Quintin only laughed again. "All right. You," he said, indicating Brenda, "get the sweaters, so we can all have dinner."

He stared at Brenda, who was staring back at him like a doe caught in the headlights of a speeding car.

"Hop to it!" Quintin said, and Brenda did.

"What about Crai—" Scooter began, doffing his coat and accepting one of David's old sweaters.

"Later," Quintin said.

"But it's freezing out," Scooter said.

"Later, after dinner."

"But—"

"What happens, happens," Quintin said.

What the hell are they talking about? Kat wondered. *Who or what is "Crai"?*

"We'll put your coats in the mudroom," Skyler said, and Kat could see that her mother was trembling as she picked up Scooter's discarded coat and tossed it into the small tiled mudroom off one side of the foyer where they were standing.

"I'll hang mine, if you don't mind," Quintin said,

suiting his actions to the words. "Now let's go. I'm starving."

He looked up suddenly, and Kat instantly backed even farther into the shadows, her heart thundering. Had he seen her? Apparently not, because he set his hand on Skyler's shoulder and repeated, "Let's go."

"Get your hands off her," David said.

Quintin seemed surprised, but he only smiled. "Just remember, everyone on good behavior. Everyone. We keep close together, like a good family, and no one gets hurt."

They left the entry hall and moved into the kitchen, and Kat was left alone with her roiling thoughts.

She felt frozen, paralyzed, but she knew she had to get past that. Her mother had kept them from knowing she was in the house for a reason: so she could save the family.

Or so she could live when the invaders massacred the rest of the family.

No. That wasn't going to happen. She would find a way to make sure of it.

She prayed silently for strength. What the hell

should she do? How was she supposed to get help in the middle of a blizzard?

She couldn't wait until the weather calmed down, because Quintin and Scooter were waiting for the same thing. Then they would no doubt steal one of the family's cars and get back on the road.

And before they went on the road...

They would kill her entire family. They hadn't hidden their faces. They had blithely offered their names. Of course, they might have made up the names they had given, but she didn't think so. The most likely scenario was that they would have dinner, savor the warmth of the house and then kill her entire family.

She turned and hurried silently down the hall to her room. She tried her cell first, but she wasn't at all surprised to discover she had no service. She hesitated, then quickly tried the landline. But either the wires were down or their unwelcome visitors had cut the lines.

Think, she commanded herself. There had to be something she could do.

She could run, but where?

Oh God, it was all up to her. And she was in a panic, failing…

She drew a deep breath.

She could not—would not—fail.

She must be in a state of delayed shock, Skyler decided. She should be paralyzed, either entirely mute or screaming, but instead she was talking, moving, almost normally. They all were, thanks to that basic instinct for survival that kicked in no matter how dire the circumstances.

The singer on the CD that had gone on playing in the background moved on to "O Holy Night." She had wanted peace so badly before but now…

Now she just wanted everyone to live.

"What the hell is that stuff?" Scooter asked, staring at one of the serving dishes.

"Bacon and cabbage, to go with the corned beef," David said sharply. Bless him, he was actually bristling at the insult to her cooking, despite the circumstances.

"Don't look like bacon," Scooter said.

"It's more like Canadian bacon," Frazier said. "It's the Irish tradition to have bacon with the cabbage."

"Cabbage is worse than bacon," Scooter said, wrinkling his nose.

"Taste it. All the flavors mix together. It's good," Skyler heard herself say as if she were coaxing a five-year-old. "Brenda, would you pass the potatoes, please?"

She could do this. They all could. It was the only way to stay alive. Because if they didn't stay calm and pull this off...

At least, she prayed, Kat would survive.

As Scooter reluctantly accepted the bowl of cabbage, Skyler dared a glance at David. His jaw was locked, a pulse ticking at his throat. His eyes touched hers, and they were filled with humiliation. He had failed to protect his family. He wanted to do something.

She shook her head. *No.*

"Hey, you're right. This shit is good," Scooter said.

"My mother does not put *shit* on the table." Jamie bridled.

There was silence for a moment; then Scooter grinned. "Sorry. It's just that...been a while since I've eaten a family dinner." He set his fork down suddenly. "I can't do this."

"You can't do what?" Skyler demanded, her heart racing. He couldn't sit and eat with them when he planned to shoot them all in a few hours?

"Leave it," Quintin said.

"Come on," Scooter protested. "The kid could be dead."

Quintin frowned, then swore in exasperation. "The kid could be a cop."

"No, he's not," Scooter insisted.

"What kid?" Skyler demanded, feeling as if she were about to explode, as if she were choking and stars would burst in front of her eyes before the total darkness of death descended.

Surely they couldn't mean Kat?

"What kid?" David breathed.

Quintin waved his fork dismissively. "Nothing for you to worry about, buddy."

Skyler was surprised to see David lean forward intensely. "Haven't you guys ever been in a blizzard before? If you left someone out there in this, he'll die. A few years ago, one poor old woman died *after* the storm. She froze to death just trying to get her mail."

Scooter looked at Quintin. "The kid is no cop," he

insisted. "I don't want anyone to die if I can help it."
Then, as if realizing that he was sounding too soft,
he added, "But don't any of you forget we've got
guns, and we'll use 'em if we have to."

"Mom first," Quintin reminded them very softly,
and Skyler lifted her head to stare at him. He laughed
suddenly. "Look at the little lioness. You think it
would be worse if I threatened one of the children.
For you, yes. But for the kids here… You think they'd
want to go on living, knowing they got you killed?"

"Ah, it's all clear to me now," Paddy said suddenly.

"What's clear, you old Mick?" Quintin demanded.

"Why, that you were abandoned by y'er blessed
mother," Paddy said.

"I wasn't abandoned," Quintin snapped back.
"The drunken bitch died. Maybe you should watch
it, Mick. You could be next."

"Speaking of abandoning people…" Skyler cut in.
"Have you abandoned someone outside?"

Quintin grinned. "You *want* us to bring in our
buddy and put the odds even more in our favor?"

There was no way she could hide the confusion that
filled her when she added that thought to the mix.

"That's all right. You're good people," Quintin said surprisingly.

"I want to get the kid," Scooter said stubbornly.

"The food will get cold," Quintin said. "And how do you propose we get him?"

"Those two get him out of the car and carry him in," Scooter said, indicating David and Frazier. "You sit here with your gun trained on Mom and they won't make trouble."

"The wind is blowing like a son of a bitch," Paddy noted.

"So it is," Quintin said. "Go get coated up."

The blow to his head had been bad. Craig groaned, shivering, his teeth chattering. He tried to open his eyes again.

Somehow he managed to sit up so he could get a look at where they were, and his heart sank.

Oh God. He'd hoped it was just the blizzard and the pain confusing him, making him see the familiar where it didn't exist, but he hadn't been confused. What he'd seen was all too real.

This was Kat's family's country home, the one she

always joked was out in the boondocks, where people still knew one another and where they cared.

Kat.

With her music and her laughter. He could remember far too vividly the times they had come up here for weekends when her family was away, the nights they had spent cuddling on the couch, watching old movies, unable to keep their hands off each other.

Casablanca rolled across his mind. He could hear Humphrey Bogart saying, "Of all the gin joints, in all the towns, in all the world, she had to walk into mine."

Except that Kat O'Boyle hadn't just walked into his life.

He had plowed into hers.

Maybe it wasn't the house, he thought, and looked again.

Nope, it was. Painted white and black with detailed Victorian gingerbreading. The porch, the sloping yard… This was the house, all right.

Maybe they weren't here. But he knew they were. He could see lights in the windows, and in the living room, a Christmas tree strung with colorful lights.

What the hell was the matter with these people?

They lived in Boston. Why hadn't they bought a vacation home somewhere warm? Anywhere but here.

Maybe, he hoped against hope, Kat wasn't there.

No, Kat never missed Christmas with her family.

He closed his eyes, wishing he couldn't see the house. When he opened them, he thought about getting out of the car, then decided to give it another second, even though the backseat now seemed as cold as the middle of an iceberg.

Even if something had happened and Kat wasn't here, her family was inside. He'd never met them, but he felt as if he knew them. Her father, set in his ways. Her twin brother, Frazier, whom he'd at least seen when Kat pointed him out once across campus. Her little brother, Jamie. He'd wanted to meet her family. Even when she had complained about them, it had been with love.

Her parents were just so old-school, she had told him once. They had both been born in the States, but their parents had come over from Ireland, and sometimes it felt as if they had only recently come over themselves. Her father thought Mexican food was weird and sushi would kill her one day. She'd once suggested they hire a country singer at the pub, and her mother had looked at her as if she'd betrayed the nation.

They fought too much, Kat had said, even admitted that they probably should have gotten a divorce.

No, he'd told her. It was great when people believed so strongly in marriage that they made it work no matter what. He'd never told her about the way his parents had gotten divorced. They hadn't meant to hurt him, of course. They were decent people who'd gotten so caught up in their own pain that he had gotten lost in the shuffle. And then, when time had passed and some of the wounds had healed…

Then everything had really gone to hell.

He closed his eyes again, and when he opened them…

There was a face looking in the window at him.

Kat's face.

He blinked to banish the hallucination. Then he heard the door open and realized she was real.

"Craig?" she murmured incredulously. "Craig Devon?"

"Kat?" He couldn't see clearly, couldn't think clearly, but he knew he had to shake it off.

"Oh my God! What are you doing here? Did they kidnap you or—"

She broke off, staring at him. He steeled himself, feeling his heart freeze and then shatter into little pieces.

"I heard you were in jail," she said. Her voice had gone as cold as the snow around them.

Jail? He felt like laughing. She didn't know the half of what had happened.

His choice, of course. The turns his life had taken weren't the kind a man longed to share with the woman he loved. The woman he longed to have love him in return.

Kat.

So impossible.

Of all the gin joints, in all the towns, in all the world…

Damn, his head hurt and his tongue was thick, but he needed to speak and speak fast. "What are you doing out here?" he asked her. "Those bastards in your house—"

"I know," she said coldly.

"So how did you get out—"

"They don't know about me," she said.

The world seemed to steady around him. He could see her in the moonlight that glowed softly through the snow. The red fire of her hair was like a silk frame around her face, and though there wasn't enough illumination for him to really see her eyes, he knew them well. Technically speaking, they were hazel, but the word wasn't enough to describe the reality. They were green, and they were gold. Sometimes they were the sun, sometimes like emeralds. But tonight they were filled with disappointment, even revulsion.

"They didn't kidnap you, did they?" she asked.

He struggled to sit. "No. But, Kat—"

He broke off when he heard a sound, and turned to look as the door to the house opened. Scooter was there with two men. Craig squinted. Kat's older brother and her father, he had to assume. "Kat." He found the strength to grip her shoulders. "Someone's coming—one of them. So if they really don't know about you, you need to get the hell out of here. Do you understand me? Disappear."

"You're one of them."

"No…not exactly. One of them hit me and—"

"One of them hit you?" she interrupted skeptically.

"Yes, and left me out here. Now get the hell out of here!"

The men were coming down the walk. She could see them now, Scooter, her father and Frazier.

"Craig, if you're with them…"

"Please, Kat, I don't know what they'll do. Go for help."

"Go for help?" she inquired. "I barely made it to the car in this wind. See the way they're all hunched over against it? Where am I going to go, Craig? How the hell am I going to get help?"

Snowdrifts were everywhere. They were going to see her footprints, he thought, as the wind picked up, howling. Maybe the snow was blowing around enough to hide her footprints.

He roused and took hold of her shoulders again. He could see her eyes. Gold and emerald. His stomach lurched. She'd been the first really good thing in his life, and he had screwed it up. "I'm begging you to get out of here and find help before Scooter sees you."

"There is no help, Craig."

"Then hide somewhere."

"Hide?" she asked indignantly. "They have my family. I can't just run away and hide. Do you have a gun? If you have one, give it to me, damn it."

"Kat, I don't have a gun."

"But you were with them."

"Kat, I'm begging you, go!"

"Are you with them or not?"

"Kat, I…"

His head throbbed with pain and humiliation at the look in her eyes. If they caught her… Lord, if they caught her… He opened his eyes and looked up.

She was gone, vanished into the snow.

He prayed for the snow to fall faster, the wind to blow harder, to cover all traces of her escape.

Scooter and the others had nearly reached the car. The door she'd used was still open, and her prints were still obvious. With a desperate burst of strength, he dragged himself out of the car and let himself collapse into the snow, thrashing to cover her tracks, his thoughts tormenting him.

Once upon a time, he had lived in a different world. He'd been in love with a gorgeous redheaded coed. They'd saved money by eating in and watching old movies on television.

Bogie.

Bergman.

Casablanca.

Of all the gin joints, in all the towns, in all the world…

Run, Kat, run.

THREE

Everyone left in the kitchen stared at Quintin except for Uncle Paddy, who continued to eat without even looking up. "Ye've outdone yerself, lass," he told Skyler. "This is delicious. Isn't it—Quintin? That's yer name, right?"

Quintin had been staring back at Skyler and Jamie, but now he turned his attention to Paddy. "Yes, it's very good," he said.

"Thank you," Skyler said. Ridiculous. She was thanking a killer for complimenting her cooking. But they had to get through this somehow, and if being po-

lite was what it would take, then she would be as polite as if she'd been valedictorian of a finishing school.

"You spend a lot of time cooking?" Quintin asked.

"Not really," Skyler told him, and without thinking, started to rise. He tensed. "Sorry. I just thought
I'd have a beer," she said.

"I'll have one while you're up," Quintin said.

"Hell, I'll be joinin' that party," Paddy said.

Even Brenda spoke up. "Mrs. O'Boyle, I'd love a
beer, too."

"I'll just grab a six-pack," Skyler said. Poor Brenda.
The girl was probably wishing herself miles and
miles away right now.

She could have been with her own family. In fact,
Frazier could have been with them, as well.

She was the reason they were here instead. She
had subtly tried to make him feel guilty for even con-
sidering spending Christmas somewhere else. *But,
Frazier, you really should come while we still have the
house. You know we'll probably get rid of it soon, since
there's no sense keeping it now that you kids don't really enjoy it anymore. Just this year…*

Just this year. So Frazier was here with her, along with Brenda, and now they might well die with her.

Stop thinking that way, she commanded herself, but she couldn't help it. Could these men really let them live? They seemed ruthless enough to have killed already. And if you were going to go to prison for life, hell, what difference did it make just how many murders you were being punished for?

"I take it there will be dessert?" Quintin said, almost as if he were a real guest.

"Blueberry pie, apple pie, chocolate-chip cookies," Skyler said.

"Wow."

"My parents own a pub," Jamie said.

"So blueberry pie is Irish?" Quintin asked.

"It's universal, I think," she told him.

"What about pumpkin? I thought that was traditional," Quintin said.

"That's Thanksgiving," Jamie protested.

"We can have pumpkin pie for dinner tomorrow, if you like," Skyler told him.

"Sure, I like pumpkin." He frowned. "So where is this pub of yours?"

"Boston," she said.

Quintin started laughing. "You live in Boston, and this is your vacation home?"

"Hey, we could use some help over here!" Scooter shouted from the front door, interrupting the conversation.

They all leaped up and went rushing out. Between them, Frazier and David were supporting a semiconscious man, his eyes closed, his legs barely moving as they walked. The mysterious not-a-cop, Skyler assumed.

This man clearly wasn't like Quintin or Scooter, hardened and with an edge. This man was younger. Not much older than Frazier and Kat, she realized.

And he was hurt. A trickle of dried blood marred his forehead and matted his hair. Light hair. His eyelashes fluttered as he looked up at her, and for a moment his eyes went very wide, as if he knew her. As if he somehow recognized her. Which was ridiculous, she thought, because she'd never seen him before in her life.

A pained smile tugged at his lips; then his eyes closed again and his head dropped. The only reason

he was still vertical, she realized, was because her husband and son were supporting him.

He looked as if he'd fallen face-first into the snow somewhere along the way, and he was tall, even slumped between her husband and son. He looked to be about their height, and except for his present exhaustion, in excellent condition, like an athlete rather than a thief.

Really? she mocked herself. And just what did thieves usually look like?

Like the other two men. Hard, dangerous, cold—and soulless.

"Set him down on the sofa," she said.

As soon as they did so, she knelt down beside him and carefully probed the wound on his head. He cried out involuntarily, his eyes—dark blue, she saw in the light—fluttering open again.

"Hey," Scooter protested. "Don't hurt him."

"Like it makes any difference," Quintin muttered.

"I'm just trying to see how badly he's hurt," Skyler said. "I think he may have a concussion." She looked from Quintin to Scooter. "He should never have been out in that car. You could have killed him."

Her words were met with silence.

Maybe they—or one of them, anyway, she thought, remembering Quintin's cavalier attitude toward bringing him in—*had* been trying to kill him. Or else had taken the attitude that if he died, he died.

"Told you," Scooter said.

"He deserved what he got," Quintin snapped.

Deserved…

So who had cracked him in the head? Someone they had accosted earlier tonight?

Or Quintin?

"Jamie, can you get the first aid kit, please? It's up in my bathroom."

She heard a click and looked up quickly. Quintin had clicked off the safety on his gun, and his finger was on the trigger.

"I'll just get the kit. I swear it," Jamie said, staring at Quintin.

"Please," Skyler said softly. "This man is your *friend,*" she added, hoping it was the truth.

"I'll go with him," Scooter said.

"Make it fast," Quintin said. "There's still a meal on the table. And dessert."

As she listened to Jamie's and Scooter's footsteps on the stairs, Skyler realized everyone else was clustered around her. Frazier had his arm protectively around Brenda's shoulders, but his eyes were on Quintin and the gun. Uncle Paddy was standing silent, leaning on his cane. David stood as tense as strung piano wire, watching her.

The torment in his eyes was terrible to see. Worse than her fear that she would be shot. Almost as bad as her fear that her entire family would be massacred if they made a wrong move.

Or even if they didn't.

As soon as Jamie came back with the first aid kit, she found the antiseptic and bathed the cut, happy to have something to concentrate on other than her fears. He stared at her steadily the entire time.

She almost fell over when Brenda stepped forward. "I can see if there's any kind of fracture, Mrs. O'Boyle. I'm pre-med."

"That would be great, thanks," Skyler murmured, trying to hide her shock, though she did remember Frazier saying Brenda was brilliant.

"Just a concussion," Brenda said with surprising confidence a minute later. "I'm sure he'll be all right."

Skyler and Brenda looked at one another. Even Skyler knew he shouldn't be lying down on her couch. He should be in a hospital. But that wasn't going to happen. He was going to have to make it— or not—on his own.

Craig Devon.

She couldn't believe it.

Kat's mind raced. She'd made it around to the back of the house, where at least she could flatten herself against the house and get some shelter from the ripping wind. But despite the slight relief, she felt as cold inside as she did on the outside.

Craig Devon was somehow connected with the monsters who'd invaded her house.

She remembered—so clearly—the first time she'd seen him. It had been her first year of college and Craig had been just about the most gorgeous human being she'd ever encountered. It had been one of those storybook things: she'd noticed him across a crowded room, and then he had noticed her back.

Looking back—as she often had after their breakup—she realized there had been something not quite right from the start. She had been madly in love with him, so much so that she'd avoided introducing him to her twin, because she hadn't wanted Frazier going all brotherly and protective on her. She woke up each morning longing to stay in bed with Craig. She remembered all the times they'd laughed about some incident or other within her family. She'd told him all about her parents and her brothers; she'd talked about the pub and Uncle Paddy, about how much she missed her grandparents. She'd admitted hating their accent when she was a kid, because it marked them as strange, different from her friends' families, then growing up and missing them so much because they had held such a wealth of knowledge about a different time and a different place. She had been an open book.

He hadn't even been a short story.

Had he always been a criminal? she wondered now. Where had he and those monsters come from to wind up plowed into a snowbank in front of her family's country house? Had he…

Killed anyone?

She refused to believe it.

But there was no denying that he was somehow connected to the two men holding her family hostage.

She thought back to the way they had broken up. Their relationship had seemed so full of promise. He hadn't been a music major, like she was, but he had joined her and some of her bandmates often enough. He could play a guitar as well as many a weekend would-be rock star. His major had been international law, and he was a senior who'd made dean's list every semester. He'd seemed to be the type of guy who would go off and solve at least a few of the world's problems. He'd been popular and worked in the gym, helping the disabled students. He'd been…wonderful.

She recalled how sometimes, when they'd been studying, she would look up to see him watching her. He didn't move; he just watched her with the warmest expression in his eyes. Sometimes he would smile, then go back to studying. Other times he would drop his book, never taking his eyes off her. A slow, mischievous smile would curve his lips, and then the look in his eyes would become passionate. They were both young, after all.

Before Craig, her sexual experience had been limited to three awkward occasions with Pete Barrows, her high school flame. With Craig, she'd learned what it was all about. The excitement. The climax. The longing created by the look in someone's eyes, a scent, a word, a touch. He was gentle, forceful, exciting. Being with him was never awkward, but always incredible, frequently filled with laughter.

She remembered one occasion, lying naked, waiting for her heart to slow and her breath to come naturally, when he had suddenly turned to her and asked, "Hey, do you know what they rated that new pirate movie?"

"What?"

"Arr," he'd said, and they'd both laughed.

"My God, that's a horrible joke," she'd told him, but she'd forgiven him immediately when he'd pulled her into his arms and they'd made love all over again.

Her life had been perfect. She was getting good grades, having a wonderful time, and she was madly in love.

Until, out of the clear blue, he'd told her that he was changing his life, that he didn't really love her, that he was leaving right after he graduated.

She had been stunned. She'd spent a week drinking and crying, and nearly flunked out. She'd gone to his graduation, hoping… But he hadn't even shown up.

She'd been mean to her parents and ignored her brothers. She'd spent what now seemed like half her lifetime wallowing in self-pity. But finally she'd pulled herself together, refusing to allow herself to self-destruct over a guy who had turned out to be a jerk.

And now…here he was again. She could barely believe it.

He had just…walked out. On her, on his life. And why? To become a criminal?

Had he just woken up one morning thinking, *Wow, it would be great to befriend the dregs of society and start robbing people, maybe kill a few?*

She realized suddenly that if she stayed where she was much longer she was going to start suffering from hypothermia, even though she'd put on the warmest clothes in her bedroom. She had to move. She was pretty certain she could slip back into the house through the basement window—the same way she had left.

Numb, she made her way to the back door—which squeaked, which was why she hadn't dared to use it—and slipped back through the window. She made a mental note to tell her father that a robber could easily break in that way, then laughed at herself, given that they'd let robbers—or worse—in through the front door tonight.

She shivered and hugged herself, trying to both warm her body and thaw her mind, and looked around in the dim light filtering in from the stone stairway leading down from the pantry.

The basement had seemed full of promise when she first headed down. She'd been certain there would be something down there that she could use as a weapon. The yardman was always leaving his tools behind.

But not this time. The basement offered nothing but the Ping-Pong table, paddles and balls. It was swept clean. There wasn't even a broom.

But, if she'd found something, what good would it have done? There were two of them. Or three, if Craig regained a semblance of strength.

No! her mind raged. Craig knew this was her family. He would never hurt her, and he would never hurt them. Or would he? What the hell did she know about him anymore? She hadn't seen him since he had coldly broken things off and walked away.

Had he become a dope addict? Was that what had changed his life? He hadn't looked like he was on anything out there in the car. He had just looked injured. Had one of the others hurt him? Or had he been injured while attacking an earlier victim?

She crept up the stone stairs that led to the pantry and the servants' stairway in the back of the house.

They didn't have any servants, of course, but the house had been built back when there was huge money in Western Massachusetts. The size and isolation of the place—and the cost of heating it—had been the reasons her family had gotten such a good deal on the house years ago.

She had hoped to escape to the neighbors' house for help, but her nearest neighbors were at least half a mile away. In the storm, she wasn't sure that she could find her way through the forest between the properties, but if she went by the road it would be more like two miles, and she knew she couldn't last that long in this weather.

And she wasn't even sure the Morrisons would be there or that she could get in. Artie Morrison had told her father that he was buying a condo in Boca where he could head for winter, now that he and his wife were retired and the kids had moved away.

After that, the next closest place was the jewelry and antique shop, and that was certainly closed for the holiday. Mr. Hudson was sick. He had cancer. Her mother had told her sadly that he was going to L.A. for the holidays, and that sometime during January, he and Ethan, his son, would come back together and close up for good, transferring what remained of the stock out to California, where Ethan and his wife now lived. After that…

Another human being was at least five miles away.

There was no hope of driving the cars; they were in the garage and the snow had already blocked the door. She'd had high hopes for the invaders' car, which was how she'd come to discover Craig in the first place. But even if he hadn't been in it, even if she hadn't been stunned into shock, she couldn't have driven it anywhere. Its nosedive into a snowbank had left the hood accordioned. That car was going nowhere.

Obviously they intended to steal a car when the snow cleared. A car no one would need—because they wouldn't leave anyone alive....

Stop, she commanded herself. She didn't know who these men were. Maybe they were so confident of their ability to get away that they didn't care if anyone knew their names. Yes, they carried guns, but that didn't mean they would use them.

But they might. There was one dead lamp upstairs to prove it.

At least it was just a lamp. At least the scrawny bastard who called himself Scooter hadn't shot a member of her family. Yet.

Breathe, she told herself. *Breathe. Think.*

All right, so she couldn't get help because she couldn't get anywhere alive. And dead, she would do them no good at all. But she wasn't doing anyone any good hovering in the basement, either.

If only her father kept a gun.

But he didn't.

He'd never even kept a gun at the pub, joking that he and her mother might shoot each other. But the truth was, he didn't believe in guns. He didn't like them. He had always been afraid that if you drew a gun and didn't kill your enemy immediately, that gun might be taken away and turned on you or another innocent. Besides, the pub was a stone's throw from a police station.

So there was no prayer of finding a gun in the house, but how did you combat a gun without a gun of your own?

There had to be a way.

She moved carefully up to the pantry, then stood dead still, listening. Voices didn't filter back this far with any clarity, but she could tell they were all in the living room, and she could hear the man named Scooter speaking, followed by her mother. After a minute her ears became attuned to the acoustics, and she began to make out parts of their sentences.

"You took a nasty blow…head," her mother said. "I cleaned…have quite a cut there…your hairline. You…careful not to sleep for a while."

"He's all right. Dinner…getting cold," Scooter complained.

"You're the one…had…out for him," Quintin snapped.

"I could…frozen…death!"

That was Craig's voice. And he had snapped back at Quintin, apparently comfortable enough with the other man to show his anger. Her heart sank. He *was* with them.

"Let's…back to the kitchen," Quintin said.

"I need…first aid kit away," Jamie said.

"Leave it," Quintin told him.

"What should…do with him?" Scooter asked.

Him? Kat frowned, then realized with relief that he had to be talking about Craig.

"He…stay…stare…tree for a while," Quintin said.

Kat heard shuffling and people talking over each other, presumably getting Craig settled in the living room, followed by the sounds of everyone else returning to the kitchen. Without a plan—or a weapon—she knew it was time to retreat. She used the sound of their approach to cover her own escape back up the servants' stairs to the second floor.

* * *

David O'Boyle sat at his own table, completely powerless, in a fury, feeling beyond humiliation or help. He was trying with everything in him to keep his mouth shut. He was praying with the same words over and over again: God, help. Oh, God, help. God, help. Help....

He had met his wife's eyes so many times, had seen the plea in them. There was nothing they could do that wouldn't get them killed except play this game.

Great game.

Scuzzy criminals who were probably cold-blooded murderers were sitting at the dinner table. *His* dinner table. They were complimenting the food, drinking his liquor, making conversation as if they belonged there.

How the hell was he supposed to keep from throwing himself at one of them, even if it meant taking a bullet? But he couldn't take the risk that the other one would shoot Skyler or one of the kids. God help him, if there was just one of them... But there were two.

No, now there were three.

Of course, one was prone and possibly passed out

in the living room, so at the moment, he didn't count. And he was younger, maybe not as blood-thirsty. Or maybe more so.

Hell.

He looked over at Paddy.

Fuck the old bird. He was chatting away with their vicious guests as if they were long-lost comrades from Dublin, filling their glasses again and again with whiskey, and saying the same things over and over, as if he had Alzheimer's.

Filling their glasses…

Was he hoping to get them drunk?

Maybe so, and it wasn't such a bad idea, now that he thought about it. Hell, it was better than anything he'd come up with.

No heroics. Quintin had sworn that he would kill Skyler, and David had the feeling that he'd do it.

"So when did you leave Ireland, old man?" Quintin asked, accepting another shot of Skyler's best single malt.

"The summer of sixty-four," Paddy said. "I'd had it with the violence." He winked at the table. "The minute I got to the States, I decided to be a Buddhist."

"Uncle Paddy, you're not a Buddhist," Jamie said.

"He's an alcoholic. That's his religion," Frazier told Quintin and Scooter. But there was no malice in his words. He was almost smiling as he looked at his uncle.

"'Tis true. I do worship a fine single malt," Paddy admitted.

"So then you opened a pub?" Scooter asked

"No, sir, I did not. My sainted and now dearly departed sister and her husband opened the pub. I merely worked in it."

"He thought he was the social liaison," David heard himself say. But there was no malice in his voice, either.

I'm sorry I ridiculed you and wanted you out of my house, David thought. He was sorry that he'd argued with Frazier about the tree, too. He was sorry that he had so often been quick to find fault with all his children.

He stared across the table at Frazier. They might all end up dying in the hours to come. But not all of them, because he wouldn't let that happen. When the time came…

When would that time be?

He didn't know, but when it did, he would throw himself on one of the men and hope the others would overpower the second man left behind. And that someone would live.

But it wouldn't come to that for a while. Not while the wind and snow continued to rage. Not while the invaders were still being fed. Not while his family continued to entertain them.

David wanted to tell Brenda that she was welcome in his house, that he was glad she and Frazier made each other happy.

But he didn't want to draw attention to the women in his house. For all he knew, Quintin and Scooter could be rapists as well as killers. In fact, he was afraid that the only reason nothing like that had happened was because Quintin wanted two guns available at a moment's notice.

He went back to trying futilely to think of a way.

She came down the stairs in silence, a vengeful fire goddess with the red of her hair blazing against the white parka she'd found in her parents' closet.

Craig felt an instant rush of panic and looked toward the kitchen. There was no sign of anyone returning to the living room, but Quintin and Scooter knew nothing about Kat, and he was desperate for it to stay that way.

"What the hell are you doing?" he mouthed as she walked toward him.

"What the hell are *you* doing?" she mouthed in return.

"Listen—" he whispered when she was close enough to hear him.

"No, you listen. If you let them harm a single hair on the head of any one of my family, you are a dead man, do you understand?"

"I told you to get the hell out of here," he said.

He tried to sit up, but though the room swam, he resisted the temptation to go under again. She touched his face, and her fingers were soft and cool.

"You're burning up," she said, stepping back.

"Get out of here," he told her.

"I need to know—from your lips—that you're with them."

"You don't understand." He broke off when he

heard a chair scrape against the kitchen floor. They could be heading back. "Get out of here, Kat, now."

She had heard it, too, but she paused, staring at him in a way that made his insides curl. "Do you have a gun, too? Are you going to shoot someone?"

"I had a gun…. Quintin took the bullets."

"So you *are* with them," she said in disgust.

"No."

Another chair scraped back.

"Get out of here," he told her again.

That time she listened and silently disappeared back up the stairs just as Quintin came into the room.

"You're sitting up. Feeling better?" Quintin asked.

"Yeah. No thanks to you, you asshole."

"Careful. You're the asshole, and I can make you a dead asshole real easy. In fact, I *should* shoot you. That would guarantee good behavior out of this family."

"Great. Why?" Craig demanded, making sure to keep his eyes on Quintin. Not to let them wander. Kat was on the landing, he was certain. Listening. Watching, perhaps.

"Why?" Quintin demanded, as if surprised.

"Yeah. Why bother with them?" Craig asked.

"I like the food. The comfort. The warmth of the house. Hell, I even like the feeling of having a family for Christmas."

"Glad to hear it."

"What else is there to do? There's no way to go anywhere in this storm, so tonight, we're all just one big happy family," Quintin said.

"The storm will stop eventually. What then?"

"And then we leave. I may let you live then, and I may not," Quintin said.

"What about them?" Craig demanded, lowering his voice.

Quintin smiled. "What about them?"

"What happens to them?"

Quintin shrugged. "Well, tomorrow is Christmas. Not a good day for anyone to die."

"And then?" Craig persisted.

"Then," Quintin said very softly, "it won't be Christmas anymore."

FOUR

"I said, no more," Scooter muttered irritably.

"What?" Paddy demanded, waving the whiskey bottle in the air. "No more? This is the best, I tell ye, my good man."

"I said enough," Scooter said.

David was afraid that the man was really losing his temper. Although Scooter liked to talk big, Quintin was definitely the boss of the two. But Quintin was in control of himself, while Scooter was like a loose cannon.

"Scooter," he said.

The man looked at him in surprise, perhaps because David had spoken to him by name. "What?"

"He…uh…it's Alzheimer's."

Scooter frowned; then his eyes widened. "You mean the old fart's going senile."

"Yeah."

"What?" Paddy demanded indignantly. But it had been his ploy all along. A good ploy? David didn't know. But all of them were acting, and Paddy's act was as good as any other. He lowered his head for a moment.

"Nothing," David said.

"He's not crazy, he's just a drunk," Jamie said.

"A drunk going crazy," Frazier told his brother.

"I'm not drunk yet—unfortunately," Paddy complained.

"Close enough," David said, though he didn't really think Paddy was close at all. After years of pickling his brain, the old man could hold a prodigious amount of liquor.

"Everybody be nice," Skyler commanded, rising and picking up her plate. "Frazier, hand me that platter, please."

"What are you doing?" David asked.

"The dishes, obviously," she said.

Do the dishes matter when we all might be dead soon? David wondered.

He didn't ask the question aloud. As he rose to help clear the table, Quintin returned to the kitchen, along with the newest arrival.

The guy still looked a little green, but he offered what looked like a genuine smile. "I'm a little late. Mind if I grab something?"

Skyler turned to him with a smile. "Of course not. What would you like?"

That was Skyler through and through, David thought: making sure a crook didn't go hungry. They couldn't even get rid of rats at the pub in the normal way; they had to go out and buy the humane traps, then set the rodents free out in the country. Even when the rats were bigger than the alley cats that continually hung out looking for scraps.

"Are you feeling better?" Skyler asked the newcomer.

He shrugged. "I feel hungry. I think the smells coming from the kitchen gave me strength."

Just what they needed: to give the guy strength. "Sit. I'll get you a plate," David said. What else was there to do? At least this one was polite.

"Who plays the piano?" Quintin asked.

"Everyone in the family," David replied curtly.

"Do you all sit around the piano and sing Christmas carols?" Scooter demanded, laughing.

"Yes," Skyler informed him icily.

"Christmas carols, huh?" Quintin said thoughtfully. "That might be…interesting. It's not like we want to watch the news."

Ice trickled along David's spine. They didn't want to watch the news. Why not? What were the men afraid he and his family would learn about them if they were to watch the news? Or would anyone even know anything yet, with the storm at full fury?

"Christmas carols sound great," Craig said. He looked at Jamie. "Is the piano your favorite instrument now? Or is that guitar I saw in the living room yours?"

Jamie shrugged. "The guitar's mine, but I like them both."

Now? David thought. The man had said "now." As if he knew Jamie. But that was impossible…wasn't it?

"Frazier can play the piano way better than me," Jamie went on.

"Except for my dad," Frazier said. "Not to mention my mom. She's the one who usually plays at Christmas."

"She loves Christmas," Jamie supplied.

"Christmas carols, turkey…a warm house," Scooter said, almost talking to himself.

"So everyone in the family is a musician," Quintin said, frowning as he glanced at Scooter.

"Comes from owning the pub," David explained. "We didn't have a lot of money when we took it over from Skyler's parents. We couldn't afford to hire a band, so we made our own music." He looked at his wife and smiled, suddenly remembering the years gone by. Lean times, hard times, but they'd made do. Skyler had heard the old Irish songs all her life, and her light, melodic voice more than did them justice. His sons had grown up liking harder, Celtic-tinged rock. Frazier's favorite band was Black 47, and he often headed down to New York to hear them.

Suddenly David realized that Quintin was studying him with something like envy. "I wanted to play the guitar," the man said, sounding natural for the first time all night. "I sucked. Took after my mother, who couldn't carry a tune in a bucket."

"What about your father?"

Quintin shrugged. "Never knew him—never even knew who he was."

"I could teach you a few chords," Jamie volunteered.

"Yeah? Well, we'll see," Quintin said, reverting to form.

"Let's hear some carols," Scooter said.

"Music," Paddy said. "'Tis an Irish tradition, that it is. Along with a good whiskey. Drinking fine whiskey, now there's a talent that can be learned quick."

"We're going to sing Christmas carols, Uncle Paddy," Frazier said.

"You all go ahead," Skyler told them. "I'll finish up the dishes."

"We'll all stay together," Quintin said firmly.

"Fine. Then let me finish the dishes," she insisted.

"What difference do the dishes make?" Quintin asked softly, something ominous in his tone.

But Skyler spun around. "I was under the impression that you wanted a turkey tomorrow. If you want a turkey tomorrow, I have to clean up in here tonight. That's how you run a good business. You keep up."

David was stunned at the way she was standing up to Quintin. Skyler was an enigma. She always had been. She hated controversy, and most of the time she was the sweetest human being in the world, but every so often... When it came to the right way to do things, she could definitely stick to her guns.

"Fine. Everyone, up and help out," Quintin said.

Scooter wanted Christmas, David thought, and Quintin wanted turkey, which meant that, at least for now, they had time....

David maneuvered to stand next to his wife at the sink. As she rinsed the dishes and he set them into the dishwasher, he had a moment to whisper to her. "I *will* do something," he swore.

"No."

"Skyler..."

"Don't make them angry."

"Skyler..."

"They plan to kill us before they leave. I know that. But wait, please. It's only Christmas Eve, and it's still snowing. We have time."

"Time for what?"

"I don't know. But…it's Christmas."

Right, Christmas, with its tidings of comfort and joy. Only a few hours ago he had been irritable because Paddy was there, because Frazier had brought home a girl, because Jamie was holed up in his room, because they couldn't get the tree to stand straight. Now…he just wanted them all to be alive to celebrate New Year's Eve.

She stared at him with clear, level eyes. She was praying for a miracle, he realized. And who was he to deny her? Hell, he wasn't in any hurry to die.

"Help may be out there," she whispered, and left it at that. They both knew that Kat was still…somewhere.

"Sure," he said, and began to hum "Silent Night" to take his mind off the situation.

The next thing he knew, something hard was sticking into his back. It took him only a second to realize that it was the cold nose of Quintin's gun.

"Quit whispering," Quintin said coldly.

David turned around despite the gun and stared at Quintin. "What the hell do you think we could be saying that's such a big deal?" he demanded.

Quintin thought that over, then shrugged. "Are you done in here yet?" he asked Skyler.

"Just let me wipe the table and start the dish-washer," she said. "While we still have power."

"You have a generator. I saw it." Scooter pointed from across the room.

"Yes, we have a generator. And enough gas to keep us going for about twelve hours," David told him.

"I'd hate to waste gas doing the dishes," Skyler said. "We'll probably need it to cook with tomorrow."

"Time to head out to the living room. Everyone. All together," Quintin said, still holding the gun.

Brenda made a little noise, not so much a sob as an involuntary sigh.

"Don't cry," Quintin said. "I bet you can be plenty tough when you need to."

Frazier, pulling Brenda close, stared at him.

Quintin grinned. He had the power. He knew it, and he liked it. So far, he was just playing with them, but if he went after Frazier's girl…what would his son do? What would *he* do?

Together, they went out to the living room. Frazier, silent, his eyes on the invaders, sat at one end of the sofa, holding Brenda against him. Her eyes were wide, luminous with unshed tears. Jamie perched on a chair nearby, staying close to his brother. Skyler took the piano bench. Craig sat at the other end of the sofa, keeping his distance from his cohorts, who chose the armchairs near the fireplace. The better to keep an eye on the captives, David thought, or because Craig wasn't really one of them? He remembered Quintin's accusation that Craig was a cop, and he wondered.

"There are no ornaments on this tree," Scooter complained.

"We hadn't gotten to it yet," David said.

"You have ornaments, though. Right?" Scooter wanted to know.

"Of course we have ornaments," David said wearily.

"Where are they?" Scooter asked.

"In the attic. We hadn't brought them down yet," David explained.

Scooter looked at Quintin. "We need ornaments."

Quintin glowered with aggravation. "All right. Scooter, you take Dad up there and he can get the ornaments."

"They're heavy boxes," David said. "And there are a lot of them. I'll need help."

"You—go with your father," Quintin said, pointing at Jamie.

"Sure," Jamie said, but he hesitated.

"What now?" Quintin demanded.

"Frazier and Dad always bring down the boxes. My si—my mother and I pick out which ornaments go on the tree first. It's tradition," Jamie said stubbornly.

"You people and your friggin' traditions! Fine. You—" Quintin said, pointing at Frazier. "Go with your father."

Brenda clung harder to Frazier, wide-eyed and terrified.

"Brenda," Skyler coaxingly said, walking over to her. "Come over to the piano with me. We'll find some sheet music, okay?"

Brenda nodded, tried to smile and got up to join Skyler.

"I think the ornaments can wait for just a minute," Quintin said suddenly. "I want to hear something on the piano."

They all went still. David was suddenly aware of the ferocity of the wind outside the safety of the house.

Where was his daughter? Had she gone for help? Was she lying dead in the snow somewhere?

No. Kat was smart. She would know that she couldn't make it for help in this weather. Know that she would have to stay hidden, that eventually she would have to listen as they shot down her family.

Don't think that way, he told himself. *Believe.*

Believe in what? God? Miracles? One of his mother's sayings suddenly came back to him. *God helps those who help themselves.* And he *would* help himself and his family, by God. When the time was right.

Whenever the hell that was.

"Someone play the friggin' piano," Quintin snapped.

Skyler sat down, taking Brenda's hand and inviting the girl to sit next to her on the bench. She trailed her fingers over the keys, and David knew she was thinking about what to play.

She started singing "We Wish You a Merry Christmas," and David thought again that this was beyond bizarre, his family and the men who would probably kill them sitting around the piano on Christmas Eve.

To David's amazement, Jamie walked over to the piano and started singing, too. Then Frazier joined in, followed by Brenda, and David realized that somewhere along the way he'd started singing himself.

And so had Scooter.

The house was warm, everyone was full after dinner, the music was good, and this felt ridiculously like a warm family scene.

When Skyler finished the first song, she went into "O Little Town of Bethlehem." From there, she sang about the little drummer boy, letting Jamie take the lead. Uncle Paddy backed him up with his fine Irish tenor.

When the song ended, Craig clapped, Scooter followed suit, and even Quintin smiled.

"We should get the ornaments now," Scooter said eagerly. "And she should keep playing," he announced, pointing at Skyler.

"All right," Quintin said.

Skyler immediately started playing a rousing rendition of "Rudolph, the Red-Nosed Reindeer."

Tears were streaming unnoticed down Kat's face as she sat on the second-floor landing, listening, paying attention to every word, every nuance of tone.

She knew she couldn't leave. She wouldn't make it even a quarter-mile, much less the distance she would need to go. She had to wait for the weather to subside. The problem was, that was when the killers would be ready to leave, too, and before they did...

She was also afraid to leave. Afraid something terrible would happen if she did.

She was her family's only hope for survival, and she didn't know what to do, so she listened to the music and let her mind wander, hoping her subconscious would provide an answer while the rest of her mind was distracted.

Christmas carols were a family staple at the holidays. They could argue among themselves until they were ready to tear each other's hair out, but the fighting stopped when it was time to gather around the piano.

She felt a surge of fury. Those *monsters* were gathered around *her* piano in *her* home, threatening *her* family as her mother played the piano.

She was still in her parka, afraid to get caught without it, though she had unzipped it because the house was warm.

Warm and cozy, smelling deliciously of dinner and the bayberry candles her mother had set out. It always amazed her. They came here so infrequently and stayed so briefly, but this place had become a true holiday home for them. In a matter of hours they always managed to get their act together, despite all the bickering.

She felt a lump in her throat, a rolling in her stomach. Craig Devon—the tall, blond, muscular Mr. Gorgeous she had once loved—was down there with her family. The family he knew so much about because she had told him so much about them, while he'd told her nothing about himself.

Because, despite his boy-next-door looks, he was nothing but a criminal.

How had he gone from being a man filled with promise to what he was now? As she stared down at him, her nausea threatened to spill over. She remembered reading about a rash of heists conducted by thieves who hit small jewelry and antique shops throughout the Northeast, mainly in rural areas and mostly at night. And Hudson's, she thought now, was so close to this house. Police had warned that the thieves might be armed and very dangerous. One article had said police were searching for the killer or killers of a night watchman at a bank, who had been found dead near one of the jewelry stores, although they felt it was an unrelated incident. But what if it had been related after all?

If these men had killed before, they would certainly be willing to kill again.

If...

Maybe they hadn't killed the night watchman.

Right. There was a heist, and there was a dead man, but some passing maniac had done it.

That had been in New Hampshire. *Live free or die.* Apparently they had taken the state motto to heart.

She shifted slightly, gritting her teeth, and tried hard to remember any other details. As she moved, she felt her worthless phone in her pocket. She pulled it out, thinking that it couldn't hurt to see if she could get a signal.

She swore silently at the no-signal message, then stared in disbelief when the phone flickered for a moment and went dead. As she stared at the traitorous cell, she heard the music stop and people start talking about going up to the attic.

She scrambled to her feet, knowing that, whatever she was going to do, she had to move fast.

"Ready?" Scooter asked David.

"Sure," David said. "Frazier, let's go get those boxes down."

"Wait a minute," Quintin said. "What else is up in that attic?"

Skyler stopped playing and turned to answer him. "We don't have a gun up there, if that's what you're afraid of," she said flatly.

Quintin actually grinned, shaking his head. "Bleeding-heart liberal, huh? Guns don't kill, buddy. People kill," he said.

"Thanks. I'll remember that," David told him.

"You don't hunt, I take it?" Quintin said.

"No, I don't hunt."

Quintin shrugged, as if David were only half a man.

"Some men don't need to hunt," Skyler said, staring at Quintin. "They don't need guns."

Quintin laughed. "Well, right now, I've got the gun, and that makes me the man to watch, doesn't it?"

"Skyler…" David said soothingly.

"I've got the gun, and if I want 'em, I've got the cute little blonde, your wife and your sons," Quintin said to David. "And that makes me feel very important."

"Let's get the ornaments, Frazier," David said tightly.

"Scooter, watch them," Quintin warned.

"Quit acting like I'm a damn idiot," Scooter snapped.

"You're not an idiot, you're like a fucking little kid, wanting to decorate the Christmas tree," Quintin retorted.

"Hey!" Craig spoke up. "Cut it out, you two. Quintin, the tree and the music are nice."

"Why the hell not have Christmas?" Scooter demanded.

Quintin narrowed his eyes. "Fine, let's have Christmas." He turned to David. "Just don't do anything stupid up there and make me shoot your wife. Or even Blondie over there."

Brenda gasped.

"Oh, shut up," Quintin commanded.

"It's all right," Skyler said, putting her arm around the girl as they sat on the bench.

"I'm just going to get the ornaments," David said. "That's all."

Scooter had his gun out, and he used it to gesture toward the stairs. "I'll be right behind you guys," he said. His tone was pleasant and yet somehow disturbing.

David headed for the stairs, walking heavily. If Kat was still in the house, listening, watching, she needed to be warned.

Don't do anything foolish, Kat, he prayed silently. You have to live.

He heard his son behind him, and Scooter behind Frazier. When they reached the upstairs hall, he pulled down the ladder to the attic and started up.

"No tricks," Scooter warned.

"No tricks," he promised wearily.

He couldn't think of a trick that could save them.

Not now. Not when Quintin was holding a gun on the rest of his family.

A thought raced through his mind. What if they could disarm Scooter? At least Frazier might have a chance to live.

And he would know his life had been at the cost of his family and the woman he loved.

"Don't get too close to your father, kid. Let him hand you the boxes," Scooter said.

"I have to stand at least on the second rung to reach," Frazier told him.

"Yeah, yeah, all right. Hurry up," Scooter said nervously.

So Scooter was the nervous type, David thought. Maybe if they learned more about the three men, it could be useful.

He grabbed one of the ornament boxes and turned to hand it to Frazier. His son's eyes met his, and David realized that for once, his son was looking to him for a lead.

He offered a smile and tried to fill it with the assurance that that they would get out of this somehow.

Frazier nodded, and David found himself mentally

listing his sons' strengths. Jamie was young and thin, but tall, strong and perceptive. Frazier was always at odds with him, but he was strong, bright and a creative thinker. They might not have any options right now, he thought, but the time might come, if they could just stay alive until then.

Stay alive—and pray their captors would make a mistake.

There were three of them now, including Craig, the injured one. But was he as much of a danger as the others? Hard to tell. Just how injured was he, anyway? He would bear further watching. He was with the criminals, but there was definite tension there. Maybe that was the answer: playing them against each other.

"Should Frazier take that one on down?" David asked.

"What do you mean? You planning something?" Scooter asked suspiciously.

David almost laughed. "I wish I had a plan. Should he take that box downstairs now, then come back so I can hand him the next one? Or do we all walk downstairs and back up again with every box?" he asked.

Scooter scowled, then turned to Frazier. "Take that

one down and get right back up here. And you," he said, indicating David with the nose of the gun. "Don't make a move until the kid is back up here. Any tricks, kid," he said, returning his attention to Frazier, "and I put a hole through your old man's chest."

"Unfortunately, I don't have any tricks," Frazier said.

David knew when Frazier reached the living room with his box. Both he and Scooter could hear Quintin's explosion.

"Scooter!"

"What the fuck?" Scooter demanded, going to the rail.

"You let the kid walk down here alone!" Quintin raged.

"I have a gun on his dad, and you have a gun on his mother and his girlfriend," Scooter said. "He's just bringing the box down and coming right back up."

David could hear Quintin muttering. Scooter stared back at him, and he had to prevent himself from smiling. "Quintin really runs you on a tight rope, huh?" he asked.

"Quintin doesn't run me."

"Sure he does."

"Shut up. We work together. No one runs me."

"Sure. Whatever you say."

"Here comes the kid. He's back. Get another box, and then get down from there. You're done."

"Sure." David stepped up into the attic again. Frazier was back on the second rung below him, ready to take the next box of ornaments. David reached for the box and just barely kept himself from gasping aloud.

Kat was there.

She was three feet away, shoving the box silently over to him with one hand and putting a finger to her lips in the age-old signal to keep silent. "I can't get away," she breathed so quietly that he could barely hear her. "And my phone is dead."

He nodded to let her know he understood, then mouthed the words, "Charger in my top bedside drawer."

"I love you," she whispered, and his heart soared.

"I love you, too."

"What the hell's taking so long?" Scooter demanded.

"Nothing. I'm just getting a grip on it," he said. He stared at his daughter for a long moment, then smiled with encouragement and breathed, "Be careful."

She nodded and slipped into the shadows as he climbed down and handed the box to Frazier.

"That's it, all right?" David said, using irritation to cover his relief at knowing Kat was still alive.

"Yeah, yeah." Scooter waved the gun. "Go on, both of you, downstairs. Listen. Your old lady is playing 'Deck the Halls,' so let's go deck 'em."

FIVE

It was insane, Skyler thought. There they were, all gathered around the old piano, just like the quintessential Christmas family. But in reality it was the most terrifying situation she'd ever known. Despite that, as if trying could somehow make it real, she found herself racking her mind for the most cheerful Christmas carols possible. "Frosty the Snowman," anything with a bit of a lilt. Meanwhile, Jamie chose ornaments and handed them out. Brenda had somehow found her courage and was helping. The room was cozy and smelled of the bayberry candles she loved, along with the faint scent of dinner.

It couldn't have looked more like Christmas, at least as long as she ignored Craig, who was sitting on the sofa, watching and still looking a little green around the gills.

Her panic had subsided, hovering in the background and only rearing its ugly head occasionally, when she let herself think about what was really going on.

Suddenly her attention was caught by a loud laugh. It was Scooter, who seemed to have the time of his life, helping to decorate the tree.

"These are great ornaments," he said to Jamie. "Are they Irish?"

"No, just from Macy's," Jamie told him.

"And this one?" he asked, holding up a red tear-shaped glass ornament.

"That's an old one," Frazier told him. "From my grandparents, right, Mom?"

"Yes. It's part of a set my parents brought over from Ireland," Skyler said between songs. She took a moment to look over at Quintin, who was listening without expression. What the hell was going on in that man's mind? she wondered, then tried to figure out just how many more Christmas carols she knew.

She started to sing "What Child Is This?" the Christmas version of "Greensleeves." When she dared a look at Quintin, his eyes were almost closed, and he seemed strangely at peace.

"Do you know any Irish carols?" Quintin asked when she'd finished.

"Does a bear shit in the woods?" Jamie demanded. "Sorry, Mom."

She shrugged. She'd heard the word before. Sad enough to say, she'd probably used it herself, even in front of her children.

"Do you want to hear more Christmas music," she asked Quintin, "or just music in general? Jamie could get his guitar." She looked at Frazier. "And we could do with a violin."

"Yeah," Quintin said. "Yeah, that would be nice."

They all stared at him.

"The boys' instruments are upstairs in their bedrooms," Skyler said.

"Go with them, and keep the gun on them," Quintin told Scooter.

"Why?" Scooter demanded. "The kids know if they do anything, Mom gets it right between the eyes."

In the end, Skyler thought with a moment's panic, Mom will get it between the eyes anyway. David and I need to just throw ourselves on top of these guys and hope the kids can…

No, not yet. They had all night. The storm was still freezing everything in their little world. There was time.

"Go with them," Quintin insisted to Scooter.

Suddenly Craig spoke up. "I can do it."

Quintin looked at him, a strange, twisted grimace on his face. "But you're not armed, are you?"

"Scooter can give me his gun. You don't need two of them down here."

"I don't think so," Quintin said, staring at Craig.

Craig shrugged, as if it made no difference to him. "Whatever."

Scooter let out a sound of aggravation. "Next time, you do it," he told Quintin.

"Just get going," Quintin said flatly.

Scooter stared at Jamie and Frazier. "Come on."

To Skyler's surprise, Quintin looked from David to

her after the others left and said, "This is really nice, this whole family thing, the music." Without warning, his eyes hardened. "So don't go ruining my good mood, okay?" He turned to Brenda then. "What about you? You play an instrument? Or do you just sit around looking pretty?"

Skyler put an arm around the girl. "Brenda is premed."

"She's going to be a doctor?" Quintin started to laugh.

"What's wrong with that?" Brenda asked him, surprising Skyler by speaking up so firmly.

"Are you tall enough to reach the operating table?" Quintin asked.

"She's not just tall enough, she's smart enough," Skyler snapped.

"Why don't you leave them alone?" David asked, his tone low, his words spoken with a tremendous dignity that squeezed Skyler's heart.

"I could," Quintin mused. "But I don't want to. And hey…I've got the gun."

Skyler rose and, hands on her hips, stared at the man who was destroying her family. "Brenda is at the top of her class. One day, when you've been shot and there's a bullet lodged in your brain, she could be the doctor operating on you. She plans on making something of herself. That's more than what some people here can say."

David stood, and she knew she had frightened him, that he was afraid Quintin would retaliate violently.

"Sit down, both of you," Quintin said patiently. "I'm just an old chauvinist—sorry. The kid is smart? Good for her. Are you and the boy engaged, then?" he asked Brenda.

"No," she said.

Quintin turned to David. "And you don't mind them shacking up in your house?"

David stared back at Quintin. "Yes, I mind. But I love my son, and I respect Brenda."

"Still, it's not like it was when you were a kid, huh?" Quintin said.

"No," David agreed flatly. "Times change."

"That they do," Quintin said, and though his voice was quiet, there was menace in his tone. "That they do."

* * *

Kat, who'd been watching from the second-floor balcony, leaped up lightly and fled as soon as she saw Scooter and her brothers coming up the stairs.

She raced to her room, grabbed the phone from the charger and leaned against the closed door, her heart racing as she tried to listen to what was going on.

While she listened, she punched buttons frantically and tried to send out a 911 text message, but whether or not it got through, she didn't know.

Not that it mattered. Until the storm abated, no one could get here anyway, she thought, then went back to eavesdropping.

"Come on, come on," Scooter said, as he ushered the two boys along the hall. "He just has to have his damn music, so let's just get the damn fiddle and be done with it."

"You have something against violins?" Frazier asked belligerently.

"Calm down and don't be a jerk. You're just like Dad," Jamie accused him.

"I'm not like Dad!" Frazier denied heatedly.

"Oh yeah? You get pissed off every time someone

is late. But then you're late to everything, and you say it's because you think everyone else will be late."

"Who are you to talk? Ever since you got that car, you never even show up for family occasions half the time."

"That's because I'm stuck with them *all* the time," Jamie reminded him.

"Because you're sixteen," Frazier told him.

"At least you're a twin. You always had Kat around. I have to deal with Mom and Dad all alone."

"You have a twin?" Scooter asked Frazier suspiciously. "Where?"

Against the wall, Kat sucked in a breath and held it.

"She escaped," Frazier said quickly.

"Escaped?" Scooter echoed.

"Escaped the family this Christmas. Which is exactly what I should have done," Frazier said quickly.

Their voices faded as they walked farther down the hall. When she could tell from their footsteps that they were outside Frazier's room, Kat dared to open her door and peek around the jamb. Her brothers were looking her way, and their eyes grew big when they spotted her. She shook her head in warning, and they nodded almost imperceptibly.

She held up her phone and mimed dialing, hoped they understood, then mouthed, "I love you," and slipped back inside her room, shutting the door carefully. A moment later she heard them coming back down the hallway.

Suddenly the phone clutched in her hand let out a beep. She froze.

"What was that?" Scooter demanded, and she realized he was right outside her door.

"What?" Jamie asked.

"That noise," Scooter said.

"What noise?" Frazier demanded, sounding impatient. "This is an old house. It creaks and groans all the time."

"It wasn't any fucking old-house sound," Scooter snapped. " It was a beep. Now come back here and open that door."

Frazier did his best to stall. "That door?"

"What are you, stupid? Yes, *that* door. Open it."

Kat could hear their voices, even though she had dived into her closet and hidden as best she could behind the clothes, scrunching into a corner and pulling an old comforter over herself.

"Get in there," Scooter snapped to Jamie and Frazier.

Her heart pounding, afraid her every breath was a thunderous gasp, Kat cowered as far back as she could go and listened.

"Don't you two pull anything," Scooter warned.

"What are we going to pull?" Jamie demanded.

Kat heard a thump and realized Scooter had gotten on his knees to look under the bed.

"What the hell do you think you're going to find?" Frazier demanded.

"Whose room is this?" Scooter asked, ignoring Frazier's question.

"My sister's," Jamie said. "When she bothers to show up."

"But she didn't show up?" Scooter asked.

"Have you seen her?" Frazier asked in return, sounding aggravated by the question.

"She's in love," Jamie said. "She went away with her boyfriend."

"Yeah?" Scooter said, doubt still evident in his voice.

"Will you hurry up and look wherever you're going to look?" Frazier queried impatiently. "Your crazy friend is down there with my family and my girlfriend, and he's going to start thinking something's wrong if we don't get back."

"Open that closet door," Scooter said.

Jamie snorted derisively. "Why? You think the bogeyman is in there?" he asked.

"Do it!" Scooter yelled. He sounded tense and on the edge of hysteria.

The door opened.

"Nothing here," Jamie said impatiently, although he had to know she was there.

She heard footsteps on the floorboards outside her refuge. Scooter?

"I heard something," Scooter snapped.

"I bet I know what it was," Jamie said. "You must've heard one of the smoke detectors. The battery's probably going or something."

"A smoke detector?" Scooter said doubtfully.

"Yeah, look. There's one right there. On the ceiling."

"I dunno," Scooter said. "Make it beep again, kid."

"I don't know how to make it beep," Jamie argued.

"Then figure it out," Scooter said. "Figure it out."

* * *

Quintin rose, his gun in his hand.

David stayed seated and did his best to remain calm, but the other man had a firm grip on his weapon, and it was clear that he knew how to use it. He'd used it before, David was certain. There was something in the man's eyes. A coldness. A complete lack of conscience.

He liked to be amused. Entertained. And right now they were entertaining him. He didn't want to think what would happen when that stopped.

Quintin was starting to look nervous, David realized. The others had been upstairs for what felt like a long time.

Maybe Craig had picked up on the same thing, because he suddenly said, "Quintin, you want me to go see what's going on?"

Quintin flashed him an impatient glance. "No."

"What the hell do you think I'm going to do? I'm half-dead and I don't have a weapon. I'll just go up and see if Scooter needs help."

"Go to the foot of the stairs," Quintin said, "and just yell for him."

Craig nodded and got up. "Yeah, sure. Hey,

Scooter!" he yelled when he'd reached the stairway. "What's going on?"

"He's being a jerk!" Jamie shouted from above.

David felt his stomach lurch. *Please, Jamie, for the love of God, watch your mouth. We're playing a dangerous game.*

"Hey!" Scooter objected angrily.

Craig glanced at Quintin, frowning.

Jamie appeared on the landing. "He thinks I can make the smoke detector beep again," he called down.

A beep? David thought. *They'd heard a beep? It had to be Kat's phone.* He didn't know whether to feel hopeful or even more terrified.

"Hey, Scooter, get back down here," Craig called.

He was gripping the banister to stay upright, David realized. He didn't look well, but he was basically fit, and he was still on his feet, despite being hurt and then left out in the car.

Scooter had defended Craig, David mused. And Quintin didn't trust him. He filed that information away for later.

Scooter appeared at the top of the stairway, the

boys in front of him, and looked down. "Do smoke detectors beep?" he asked Quintin.

"Of course they beep," David answered. He hoped he had just the right note of impatience in his tone.

"Do they?" Quintin asked him.

David frowned, hoping he was a decent actor. His pulse was pounding, and he realized that Quintin might not have to kill him, because he felt ready to have a heart attack all on his own. "A smoke detector beeps when you need to replace the battery," he said.

"Then why isn't it still beeping?" Scooter asked loudly.

"Because the battery beeps slowly at first, to warn you," David answered.

"Did you look around up there?" Quintin demanded.

"Of course," Scooter said.

"And?"

"I didn't find anything."

"Then get back down here."

"All right. One more minute."

David swallowed hard. Was Kat about to be discovered? And that beep...

Had her phone *worked?*

Knowing he had to do something, David got up and started to walk toward the stairs.

"Where the hell are you going?" Quintin demanded.

"Upstairs."

Quintin shook his head. "You stay right here."

"Look, I know what the problem is. I can show Scooter, so you two don't have to be worried about anything going on."

"I'll go," Craig said.

"What? Are all you people deaf or just stupid? I said you stay here," Quintin snapped.

David forced himself to sit back down calmly, then looked over at Skyler. She looked scared, her eyes too wide as they met his. He hoped Quintin wouldn't notice and realize something was going on.

She must have realized the danger, too, because she looked away and trailed her fingers over the piano keys. "Come on, guys, hurry up," she called. "It's time for Irish music."

"Oh, Danny boy, the pipes, the pipes are calling…" Uncle Paddy began.

* * *

Scooter was prowling around the room again. Kat could hear him from her hiding place in the closet.

"Please, come on," Jamie begged, real fear in his voice. "Didn't you hear him? Your friend is starting to sound dangerous."

"Starting?" Scooter said distractedly. "He always sounds dangerous. He is dangerous."

"So let's get down there."

"I'm telling you, I heard something beep."

"What? You think we have a bomb?" Frazier demanded.

"I think something's…not right," Scooter said.

"Please," Jamie begged. "Can we just go back downstairs?"

Kat willed herself to be perfectly still. She prayed her heartbeat wasn't as loud as it sounded to her own ears.

The floorboards creaked as Scooter kept walking around her room. It felt like forever, though it was certainly only seconds, before the closet door was flung open once again and he started pushing the hangers around.

Any second now, he would find her, and then they would all be dead.

Kat could almost feel him as he reached for the comforter on top of her. She felt the pressure as his fingers closed around it, and then she heard a scream as the entire house was pitched into darkness.

The power had gone out at last.

in much to supply heat for this particular sheriff's office out in the country. They were small and located in an area where there was seldom trouble, so they were expected to run on a shoestring.

There was only one person answering to her tonight: Tim Graystone. Tim had managed to pull the Christmas Eve gig by being their newcomer. Young and raw, only on the job for a month. And honestly, it wasn't as if his inexperience mattered. This area was sparsely populated and too far east to share the crimes that faced their neighbors in ski country, where an abundance of tourists made an appealing target for theft. And they were too far west to run into the troubles that Springfield, with its larger population, had to deal with.

Then again, Sheila had learned in her twenty years of duty, anything could happen. Three years ago, Barry Higgins, as mild mannered as they came under most circumstances, drank too much and shot up the civic center, killing his own minister in the process. In '95, Arthur Duggan had murdered his wife. That had been sad, but bound to happen. The best minds and hearts in social services had tried to

SIX

"Hell of a night," Deputy Sergeant Sheila Polanski said, rubbing her hands together in a vain attempt to warm them.

The power at the sheriff's office had gone out long ago. They had switched over to their emergency generator smoothly enough, but since everything was run at taxpayer expense, the emergency generators didn't allow for much heat.

And they called it *Tax*achusetts.

Hell, she called her beloved home state Taxachusetts herself, but even so, the state budget didn't kick get her to swear out a warrant against her husband, not to mention leave him. They'd told her over and over again that he would kill her one day, and finally he had.

But those were the only two violent crimes that had ever come their way. So even though they were a skeleton crew, it didn't seem likely that young Tim would have much to deal with tonight. The phone and electric lines were down, and the storm continued to rage. There wasn't much for them to do other than sit around and bitch about the weather.

Tim grinned. He was a good-looking fellow, just turned twenty-seven. Despite a hitch in the service, he'd gone through the academy and college before joining the force here, reporting to Sheriff Edward Ford. All told, there were only twelve officers working the county, six by day and six by night, though the schedule didn't mean much, because they were always subbing for one another. Edward, as the boss and the only duly elected official, usually stepped up to the plate and took Christmas Eve duty, but he had just remarried and the new Mrs. Ford, though forty, had decided to procreate. So Edward and his bride were already checked into one of the many offshoots of U Mass Medical, awaiting the new little Ford.

As a result, Sheila was working with Tim tonight. He was working here because, after his time in the service, he had come home to find his father dying of heart disease, leaving his mother alone to raise his much younger sister. He'd decided to stick around to guide her through the teenage years and throw some financial support his mother's way. Sheila didn't warm to just anyone, but Tim, she liked.

If she'd ever been able to have kids, she would have wanted one like him. But she hadn't been able to, and her husband had left her because of it.

She sat down, though she had been pacing back and forth to keep warm. Tim might have been living in warmer climes for the last few years, but he didn't seem to feel the cold. He was seated at a desk, his fingers laced behind his head and his feet propped up.

"Met any women up here yet?" she teased.

He shrugged. "A few. How about you?"

"How about me what?" Sheila asked.

"When are you going to get remarried?"

"Tim, look at me. I'm sixty-two years old, and I look like a mop. Bone thin, and my hair's gray and frizzy."

"You've got great blue eyes," he said, then leveled a finger at her. "And we're off at six. You can sleep for a few hours, then drag your butt out of bed and come on over. My mom's an expert with a turkey."

"Maybe. You don't have a bunch of old geezers coming over to try to fix me up with, do you?"

"No—and I'm not asking you to find anyone for me, either. Just a nice Christmas dinner."

She shrugged.

"You're coming?"

"Sure," she said, then jumped as Tim dropped his feet to the floor with a thump and sat up straight to stare at the computer screen.

"What is it?" she demanded.

"Look at that," he said.

Their emergency phone lines went straight to the computers once the power went down and the generators kicked in, though it was a makeshift system that only let them receive calls, not respond or call out. Now they both stared at the screen, which registered a text message sent from a cell phone.

Help. Emergency. 225 Elm.

"Two-two-five Elm," Tim said.

"The O'Boyle place. They always come up from Boston for the holidays. This had better not be another damn prank like the one their kid pulled last year."

Tim looked at her. "I suppose there's no chance we can—"

"Wait to check it out? No such luck. Bundle up, buddy. Duty calls."

"Okay," Tim said, masking his reluctance. "But how the hell are we going to get way out there?"

Suddenly the computer pinged and another message came through. The voice was tinny through the cheap speakers, but the worry in Ethan Hudson's voice was clear as he asked them to check on his father, who had stayed late at his shop and never made it home.

"Poor guy probably plowed into a snowbank," Sheila said. "Somehow, we've got to get out there. At least they're both in the same direction."

There was silence after the scream, a silence so complete and acute that Kat could almost taste it, like something metallic in the air.

This was it. The opportunity they needed.

And her brothers took it. She heard Scooter cry out as someone grabbed him, then long moments ticked past, punctuated by grunts and shuffling.

Then the generator kicked in.

She realized that what had seemed like forever had in reality been only a matter of seconds, and she cursed the generator they had begged their father to buy, though she had no idea whether the outcome would have been the same without it.

She was still in the closet when the dim light from the hallway showed her Scooter on the floor of her bedroom, Frazier straddling him and Jamie sitting on his feet.

There was a bruise darkening on Frazier's face, but Scooter looked the worse for wear, as well, with a bloody lip. And his gun was on the floor.

Jamie made a dive for the gun, reaching it before Scooter could reclaim it.

"Hold it on him, Jamie...." Frazier cautioned.

Jamie held it. Pale as a ghost, he held it.

Frazier got quickly to his feet. Scooter, wary, stayed where he was, nervously eyeing the gun.

"You don't even know how to shoot that thing, boy," he said.

"Aim and pull the trigger, that's what I'm thinking," Jamie said.

By then Frazier was next to him. "Give it over, Jamie."

Jamie passed the gun to his brother without a word.

"Get up," Frazier ordered, flipping off the safety. "Slowly. I don't want to kill you."

"No? Why not?" Scooter asked calmly.

Too calmly, Kat thought. Didn't he care if he lived or died? Shouldn't his survival instinct kick in?

"We're going downstairs, slowly, calmly, with you in front of me. And no tricks," Frazier said.

"Okay," Scooter said, and started walking toward the door.

Kat was planning to scramble out of the closet, but Frazier shook his head in warning as he passed, so she stayed silent and watched them leave the room before she crept free of her hiding place.

She was immediately grateful for her brother's caution when a second scream sounded, followed by the explosive thunder of a shot.

* * *

The darkness, sudden and total, took Skyler by surprise. She screamed and leaped to her feet before freezing, terrified that if she moved, she would crash into something. Then she gasped, hearing movement—thudding and scuffling—from upstairs.

Without warning, the lights came back on as the generator kicked in.

Under cover of darkness, while she had been frozen in fear, everyone else had shifted. Paddy had his cane raised, ready to strike viciously. The problem was, he had misjudged people's positions and was about to hit her. She screamed again, at the same time realizing that David had made a leap for Quintin.

But Craig was between them. Defending Quintin from David? Or…

Sweet Lord, had he been about to attack Quintin himself?

There was no time to ponder the question. The sound of her scream had barely faded when the air was split by the deafening report of Quintin's gun. He struck out viciously with his other hand, sending Craig crashing back on the couch as David cried out hoarsely.

Then Quintin raised his gun and leveled it on Skyler, nothing but ice in his eyes.

"Mom, get back to the piano. Old man, back in your chair. The rest of you...sit. If I fire again, it will be directly at you, not into the air. And I don't miss."

He whirled on Craig. "You are one sorry son of a bitch," he said. "Maybe," he mused, "I should just finish you off, because you're worthless."

David spoke before Quintin could fire. "Good idea. Shoot him. He stopped me from reaching you," he said in a strange mocking tone.

Quintin was still for a moment. Then he lowered his gun. "All right, Craig," he said. "Maybe you're of some use after all. But remember, I'm always watching you."

In a split second, he was at Skyler's side, and she felt the cold, hard nose of his gun pressed to her ribs.

"Scooter, get your sorry ass down here!" Quintin yelled.

"The kid has a gun on me!" Scooter shouted.

"And I have one pressed into his mother's ribs." A nasty smile twisted his features. "I've killed before, kid. And I haven't got a hell of a lot to lose. Shoot

Scooter or try to shoot me, and your mom's dead. Give the gun back to Scooter, then get back down here."

"No, Frazier!" Skyler cried. "Shoot them both!" Then she cried out in fear as David instinctively moved to protect her.

Quintin moved like lightning. The nose of the gun never shifted from her side as Quintin lashed out and caught David off guard, sending him flying so hard against the wall that she could have sworn she heard the crack of his skull before he slumped to the floor.

"Dad!" Frazier shouted in anguish as he and Jamie pushed Scooter in front of them into the living room.

"He's not dead, kid, but your mother is about to be," Quintin said.

"No, please," Frazier begged, and set the gun down on the ground. Scooter immediately turned around and retrieved the weapon, then slugged Frazier in the jaw, hard.

Her son staggered back, and she jerked free from Quintin's hold, heedless of whether he shot her or not. "Don't you touch my son!" she shrieked as she flew at Scooter, who backed off in shock. Then she turned to Quintin, and the look she gave him dared him to stop her as she walked over to her husband. "David?"

He groaned softly.

"I'll get him up," Craig volunteered, and hurried over to help. Her husband wasn't a small man, and Craig wasn't at full strength, but he managed to lift David and carry him to the sofa, then lay him out where he had been himself not all that long ago.

"Okay, okay, very sweet," Quintin said. "Now let's everybody get it together here. Stay calm. Collected. Cool. I think we need something hot to drink. Maybe a little Irish coffee will put us all back on an even keel."

Skyler swallowed, and tried hard not to think about how badly hurt her husband might be. "Fine," she said and started for the kitchen.

"No, no, no. You're too dangerous. You just proved that against stupid over there," Quintin said.

"Hey!" Scooter complained.

"You let a couple of kids overpower you," Quintin told him. "How smart was that?"

Scooter flushed and looked furious—as if he might

try to deck one of the kids again, Skyler thought, and noticed that Frazier was still rubbing his jaw.

"We'll all go to the kitchen," Quintin said.

"What about my husband?" Skyler asked worriedly.

Quintin stared at David, who still hadn't regained consciousness.

"I'll watch him," Craig said to Quintin. "I saved your ass, and like you keep saying, you've got the gun. What the hell am I going to do out here with a half dea—with an unconscious guy?"

"Fine. The rest of you, let's go," Quintin said.

The room still smelled like gunpowder from the shot he had fired, Skyler thought as she turned and started for the kitchen. "Come on, kids. And, Jamie, don't even ask. You're getting cocoa. You, too, Uncle Paddy."

Kat stood silently on the landing again, shaking.

What the hell had just happened? Her brothers had bested Scooter. The confrontation should have gone their way, but instead…

That bastard Quintin! She found herself furious that Massachusetts didn't have a death penalty. She would have liked to slip a noose around the man's neck herself.

She swallowed, her thoughts racing. *What now?*

They had all gone into the kitchen, so her mother could make Irish coffee—except for her father and Craig, who were still in the living room.

Craig...

She tried to harden her heart as she crept close enough to the banister to see. His hair was too long, and his face looked thinner. Too thin, as if the last three years had been rough on him. If so, he'd deserved it.

How had he gone from being Mr. Perfect to Scuzz of the Year?

He was talking to her father, she realized. She strained to hear, but she couldn't make out what he was saying. What she *could* tell was that her father had regained consciousness, because he was saying something back.

Craig rose and started toward the kitchen.

"Hey," her father said hoarsely, quietly.

"Yeah?" Craig asked, pausing.

"Thank you," David O'Boyle said softly.

Thank you?

Why was her father saying thank-you to one of the men who'd invaded their house?

Craig went toward the kitchen. "What the hell are you doing?" Quintin demanded as he pushed open the swinging door.

"He's starting to come around. I'm going to get some ice for his head," Craig said, and then the rest of the conversation was lost as the door swung shut behind him.

Kat hesitated. Everyone except her father was in the kitchen, she realized. How long would they stay there?

Suddenly she didn't care.

She flew silently down the stairs and raced to her father's side.

"Dad?" she whispered.

"Baby, get away from here."

"But, Dad, I'm afraid for you."

"I'm all right, honey. I had hoped you'd gotten far away by now," he said, his tone hopeless.

He had hoped she wouldn't die with the rest of them, she thought.

"I… It's a blizzard, Dad."

He smiled sadly. "I know. Get back upstairs."

"Dad, I texted the cops and I think it went through," she said. "So hang in there, okay?"

"We're hanging."

They both heard the sound of someone pushing against the swinging door to the kitchen.

"Go!"

"I'm gone!"

She flew back up the stairs to her previous vantage point and watched as Craig walked over to her father with a bag of ice in his hand.

How? she wondered again. How did you go from bad jokes and the world's most charming smile to…this?

Did you hear about the three guys who headed out for a good time one night? Two of them walked into a bar.

Yeah?

And one didn't.

I don't get it.

He ducked.

They'd both laughed, and then she was in his arms, and she could still remember the way his fingers had felt, moving over her bare flesh….

* * *

Quintin seemed to be relishing his Irish coffee. "Delicious," he told Skyler, and he grinned, as if he were a welcome guest in her home and not a monster holding a gun on her family.

"Glad you like it," she said dryly. "May I please go to my husband now?"

"He's okay. The kid's taking care of him. The kid has a heart," he said, and it wasn't a compliment.

"And that's a bad thing?" she said.

"It'll get him killed," Scooter said curtly. He was seated at the table and had gulped down his own drink, all the while continuing to eye her two sons bitterly.

"Would you like another?" she asked Quintin.

"You trying to get me drunk?" he asked.

"On Irish coffee?" she inquired.

Quintin shrugged. "Sure. Make me another."

As she rose, she asked, "Would you open the door and ask your friend how my husband is doing."

"Scooter, do it," Quintin said.

"I'm not your slave," Scooter protested.

"No, you're just the idiot who almost got us killed," Quintin said pointedly.

Scooter flashed them all an angry look but rose. "I'll have another one, too," he said.

"Of course," Skyler agreed, deciding it might be a good thing to mollify Scooter at the moment. Quintin was more dangerous, but, cornered, Scooter could be very bad, she was certain. "And thank you," she added.

"Sure." He opened the kitchen door. "Hey, Craig," he called.

"Yeah?"

"How's O'Boyle?"

"He's conscious, and he seems okay."

Skyler tried not to show just how relieved she felt as she fixed more drinks.

"Can I have another hot chocolate, Mom?" Jamie asked.

"May I," she corrected.

"You can have as many as you want," Jamie answered pertly. "You're the mom."

"Jamie…"

"Yeah, yeah, *may* I? Please?"

"Of course."

She turned around. "Anybody else?"

"Indeed, I'd be pleased to accept another," Paddy said.

"Me, too, thanks," Frazier said.

Brenda was just staring ahead, seemingly lost in her own world again, after her earlier bravery. Then, to Skyler's astonishment, the younger woman blinked, looked at Frazier as if to take strength from him, and stood up. "May I go out and check on Mr. O'Boyle? I *am* planning a career in medicine, as you know."

Quintin leaned back, looking genuinely amused.

"Yeah, that's right. But you know what? I haven't got any degree, and I can tell you this. He took a thunk on the head, but he's going to be all right. He may have a headache for a while, though."

"I'll just see how he's doing," Brenda said, and started for the door.

"Wait just a minute," Scooter protested.

"Let her go," Quintin said.

"You're the one who keeps saying—" Scooter began.

"She's two inches high, O'Boyle is still dizzy and Craig is out there," Quintin said.

Scooter stood, taking the first drink from Skyler's hand. "I'm going out there, too," he told Quintin.

"You and I are the ones with the guns. Besides, you never know." He glared at Jamie. "It's the innocent-looking ones who cause all the trouble."

Jamie looked at Quintin after Scooter left the room and shrugged. "Hey, it's not my fault he was an idiot."

Quintin leaned forward. "No, it wasn't your fault. But you act up again and I shoot your mom. And that would be a pity since we all want a good turkey dinner tomorrow, don't we?"

Skyler set his cup down before him, then returned to the counter, got the other cups and placed them before Paddy and her boys.

She realized that Paddy was staring at Quintin, assessing him. Just as he had been doing ever since their house—and their lives—had been seized.

"I'm going to see how David is," she said in a tone that brooked no interference.

Quintin lifted his cup to her. "Go on. Then we'll see about sleeping arrangements for the night."

"What?"

"You'll need some sleep to cook that turkey tomorrow," Quintin said cheerfully. "We'll need blankets and pillows if we're all going to camp in the living room."

She stared at him blankly, and he started to laugh. "Did you think the family was going to go up to their nice warm beds tonight? Please, Mrs. O'Boyle. We're all going to stay together. Just like one big happy family." He smiled as if he'd just thought of something. "And I never did get my Irish music. That will go well with my drink, don't you agree?" He rose then, still grinning. "Irish music and a slumber party. What a perfect Christmas Eve."

SEVEN

"It's dying down some, thank God," Sheila told Tim as they surveyed the department's snowmobiles, which were half buried, despite being parked under a carport behind the station. "Let's start digging."

One big happy family, having what amounted to a pajama party on Christmas Eve, Craig thought, looking at the sham festivities going on around him.

Quintin was crazy, he decided. Psychotic. The man was actually enjoying this. He was playing with these people, making them enact some sick mockery of what the night should be, letting them hope that if they did just as they were told, he would let them live. But he wouldn't. As soon as he was ready to leave, he would kill them.

But what the hell else was there to do but play along and pray that the moment would come when at least some of them could be saved?

He was amazed that he hadn't given himself away when the lights had gone out. He couldn't believe Quintin had believed he'd tried to save him, not attack him.

David O'Boyle had stood up for him. And he'd done it just right.

Why?

He'd never met the O'Boyles. His relationship with Kat hadn't gotten that far before everything went to hell. And yet her father seemed to have figured out that he had no intention of killing them, that he even planned to help them—when the time was right.

Somehow they had to wrest both guns away before blood was shed. But for the moment…

Kat, at least, was still safe—somewhere. He had to pray she would remain so.

God, he loved her. Still. He hadn't seen her in nearly three years, but she hadn't changed, at least not on the outside. But inside... Inside, she was stronger. There didn't seem to be a naive bone left in her body. Or a trusting one.

He had done that to her.

"Bravo," Quintin said as the O'Boyles finished a rendition of "Silent Night" that belonged on CD.

Craig happened to look up then, and he saw her. Kat was on the second-floor landing, looking down, tears in her eyes.

Eyes that met his briefly before she realized she had given herself away and disappeared.

"Hey, what are you looking at?" Quintin demanded.

Craig turned to Quintin and said calmly, "Nothing. Just wondering where the bathroom is."

"My jaw is killing me," Frazier said flatly. "Can I quit for a while?"

"Why don't we play a game?" Jamie suggested.

"A game?" Quintin said, and again there was that awful edge amusement in his voice. *Yes, entertain me.*

The sick thing was, Craig knew they had probably all lived so long precisely because they entertained him. And, of course, because they were snowed in and Quintin wanted turkey tomorrow.

"A game," Craig said. "Like…?"

"Trivial Pursuit. We can be on teams," Jamie said.

"No more going upstairs to get things," Quintin said.

"It's under the coffee table," Skyler said.

"All right, get it out," Quintin agreed.

Craig dared to glance upstairs again, and he silently whispered a prayer of thanks when Kat was nowhere to be seen.

The storm wasn't over, but it had definitely eased up.

Kat certainly had done lots of thinking. There were ways to fight, it was true. The problem was that Quintin had been telling the truth. The next time they fought, someone was going to die.

She stood in the basement by the window, reflecting on her chances of getting out and finding help.

There really wasn't anything to think about. She might die of exposure if she went out there, but she had to give it a try, because they didn't stand a chance if she kept hiding out here. Quintin's strength—

along with the two guns, of course—was that he didn't care if his cohorts died, while her family would fight to the death for each other.

Imagine that. Dysfunctional as they were, they would always be there for each other when the chips were down. Besides, weren't all families dysfunctional?

She gave herself a shake.

There was only one way to win. And that was to take down Quintin.

Craig would never hurt them. He might have gone the wrong way. He might be scum. But she just couldn't believe he would hurt her family.

Who was she kidding? He hadn't loved her. He'd made that clear.

Something had gone wrong with Craig, terribly wrong. But no matter how wrong it had gone, she couldn't believe he would kill her or anyone in her family. She couldn't let herself believe it, because if she did, she would lose her courage, and then they would all be doomed.

But there was still Scooter. He might be weaker than Quintin in every way, but he still had a gun, which meant he was dangerous.

She hesitated, afraid. Terrified that any move she made would be the wrong one.

Then she squared her shoulders. There was only one way for her entire family to survive. Both men had to be disarmed. And for that to happen, she had to somehow reach the sheriff's office and pray someone was there.

If she was caught...

She was dead.

And she didn't want to die.

But if she just stayed here and waited and just cowered as her family was massacred...

She wouldn't want to live.

She wrapped her scarf more tightly around her neck and pushed up the window.

David looked over at Skyler and forced himself to smile reassuringly at her.

What a joke, he thought. He was supposed to be the man of the house, the protector of his family. Well, he'd been one hell of a failure, hadn't he?

But his wife wasn't looking at him as if that was the case. Strange and bitter, but true. They'd been at odds getting ready for Christmas. She'd complained for years about how hard it was to pull everything together when they went away to celebrate, so this year, he'd been ready to give in and stay in Boston, but she'd wanted to come here.

To keep the family together, she'd said. The kids might have come around for dinner otherwise, but someone would have shown up late or left early. There would have been bitching. Arguments. And by five or six, everyone would have been gone. Even Jamie, who always wanted to spend more time with his friends than his family these days.

But could you really hold a family together by force? And did the kids really want to be here? Did he and Skyler really even know each other after all these years of constantly being at odds?

And yet…

Skyler was staring at him as she hadn't in a very long time. There was so much caring and concern in her eyes. And more. A message, as if she were trying to tell him it had been a good run, and that she loved him…whatever might come.

He tried to make his eyes say something, too. He tried to tell her that they *would* survive this.

And he knew there was something else, something they both agreed on: their children were going to survive, no matter what it took.

And they both knew that Kat was still there, a hidden asset against these men.

He returned his attention to the game, trying to hide his true feelings about this insane parody of family life Quintin was making them play out.

Suddenly Quintin was on his feet. "I hear something," he said, tension in every line of his body.

"Yeah, us," Craig said, frowning.

"No. Outside," Quintin said. "Somebody's out there."

The wind was still blowing, the snow still falling, but damned if Tim hadn't gotten the snowmobiles dug out and ready to go.

Sheila, so bundled up that she doubted she would even recognize herself, took her seat, gunned the motor and took off. Tim followed right behind.

There were abandoned cars along the road. They

checked every one, glad not to find anyone frozen inside. They kept going—up a hill and across the valley—as a full moon struggled to shed its glow through the dark clouds hiding the night sky. Finally Sheila saw a shadow rising up beside the road and knew immediately what it was.

An old building that had stood there as long as she could remember, with a sign on it reading Hudson & Son, Fine Art, Antiques, Memorabilia and Jewelry.

"Hey," she shouted to Tim over her radio. "There's the Hudsons' store."

"Let's go."

He was off his snowmobile and on his way to the door before she was.

She followed him, her nose freezing, so cold that she was afraid it was frostbitten. She couldn't help but wonder what she would look like if she had to have the tip of her nose cut off. It wouldn't be a pretty sight.

When they reached the old building, the snow was piled high against the door, but that didn't seem to daunt Tim in the least. He ran back to his snowmobile in a flash, then came back with the snow shovel he had loaded on the back.

"Good thinking, kid," she complimented him, then examined their surroundings while he started to dig. What she saw made her blood run cold.

"Look," she said, pointing toward the rear of the old structure.

They both paused in silence. Lionel Hudson's huge old Cadillac was still parked and collecting snow beside the building.

"He's in there," Sheila said.

Tim redoubled his efforts to clear the door. As soon as the drift was out of the way, he tried the door. Unlocked. Struggling against the wind, he pulled it open.

They both drew their weapons, tense, staring at one another for a long moment, and then Sheila nodded. She had a feeling their guns wouldn't be necessary. Whatever evil had visited here, it was already gone.

Even so, they entered carefully, making all the right moves.

They were greeted by darkness and silence. Tim

drew out his flashlight and sent the beam skidding around the shop.

"Lionel?" Sheila asked into the void.

There was no reply.

Sheila turned on her own flashlight and walked around the counter. There was no sign of Lionel.

Tim headed toward the back of the store. Suddenly Sheila heard him gasp.

"Sheila?"

"Tim?"

She joined him and heard her knees creak as she crouched down beside him.

"It's blood, Sheila," he said.

Her heart flip-flopped. "Do you think they might have taken him hostage?" Tim asked.

She shook her head.

"Where is he, then?"

She stared at him for a long moment, then rose. She ran back outside, suddenly heedless of the dark and wind and pelting snow. She plowed her way through until she reached the old Cadillac.

"Sheila, stop," Tim said, racing up behind her.

"But—"

"There's blood on the snow," he said quietly. "I'll look."

"I've been a deputy for most my life," she told him. "I've seen it all."

"He was a friend of yours."

Was.

She swallowed.

"Help me," she said to Tim.

Together they dug away the snow with their hands and struggled with the door to the Cadillac. As soon as they got it open, she directed the beam of her flashlight into the backseat.

"Oh God," Tim breathed.

EIGHT

Quintin told Scooter to keep everyone together, then walked toward the front door and opened it. A blast of cold hit them like a ton of bricks.

"Quintin, what the hell?" Scooter complained.

"I heard something," Quintin said.

"It must have been the wind," Frazier said. "Blowing stuff around."

Quintin flashed him an angry glance, then returned to staring into the night.

There wasn't much to see. The snow was too thick.

David cleared his throat. "If you want the generator to work all night and through…through dinner tomorrow, you can't overwork it. You don't want the heat giving out, do you?" he asked rationally.

But Quintin wasn't even listening to him. "Someone's out there," he said.

Quintin turned suddenly and aimed his gun at the group. "Craig, Scooter, get your coats on."

"Come on, Quintin, you've gotta be joking," Scooter complained.

"I'm dead serious," Quintin said, nodding meaningfully at Skyler.

"What do I care if you shoot her?" Scooter grumbled.

"What'll you care, doing life in prison?" Quintin said. "Anyway, Mr. Softie there will care."

Swearing, Scooter headed for the closet. Craig followed suit. As he buttoned his coat, he turned to Quintin and asked, "What the hell are we looking for?"

"Someone is out there," Quintin said.

"How the hell could anyone be out there? They'd be frozen by now," David pointed out reasonably.

Quintin stared at him coldly, then turned to Skyler. "Mom, come over here. Now."

David tensed as if he were about to move.

"I told you, I'll shoot her next time," Quintin said very softly.

"Just chill, everyone. It's fine," Skyler said, walking over to Quintin. He pulled her against his side and slipped an arm around her. It wasn't an affectionate gesture. He held her with the muzzle of the gun pointed to her cheek.

"Get out there," Quintin said coldly. "And if either one of you tries to pull anything, just remember that Mom here will end up with half her head blown away. Got it?"

Craig followed Scooter to the door, figuring Scooter still had a gun.

"Lookit all this damn snow. What the hell are we supposed to do?" Scooter muttered to him.

Craig shrugged. "Plow our way through it," he returned, his heart thundering. Kat had to be out here. But the snow was so deep, there would be no way to hide the trail she'd be making through the deep, white blanket that surrounded the house. And if Scooter found her... "Look, we'll just stay out here long enough to make Quintin think we really searched. Hell, Scooter, David was right. No one could survive out here."

He thought they were making their way down the front walk to the road, but it was difficult to tell. The wind was still high and flakes were still falling, and that combined with the depth of the snow on the ground made it almost impossible to tell where they were.

"Listen!" Scooter said suddenly.

"To what?"

"A motor."

"You hear a motor?" Craig said. He tried to make his tone incredulous, but he could hear it, too.

It wasn't coming from anywhere near the house, though. It was distant, the sound carrying unnaturally because of the wind.

"What the hell do you think it is?" Scooter demanded tensely.

Craig shrugged. "It's nowhere near here," he finally said, as if he'd only just managed to hear it.

"You sure?" Scooter stared at him.

Scooter had been the one to want him in the group, he reminded himself. Unlike Quintin, Scooter trusted him, and he could use that to his advantage.

"Scooter, listen," he said calmly. "It's probably just a fire engine or an ambulance or something. No one is coming to this house. There's no reason for them to."

"There's the car," Scooter said.

"Buried now. No one can see it."

Scooter stood there, staring at the moon as it tried to peek down through the heavy cloud cover. Snowflakes fell on his gaunt face and stuck to his eyelashes. After a moment he smiled. "I don't want trouble tonight," he said.

"I know. It's warm and comfortable in there. And the food's good."

"I like having Christmas," Scooter said. "I never had Christmas when I was a kid. I never knew who my dad was. And my mom…she drank. And then there were the men. She'd rather buy a gift for any asshole she thought might marry her than for her own kid." He looked at Craig. "None of her men ever stayed around, though, so she drank herself to death. And there was never Christmas until I made my own. First year after the old lady was dead, I hit up one of those department-store places. I stole a tree and all kinds of ornaments. But I got caught, and I was old enough to do real time. Haven't had Christmas since then. What about you, kid?"

"Me?"

"Did you even know who your dad was?"

"Oh, yeah. I knew who he was."

"And your mother?"

Craig shrugged, looking away. "She died young."

"She drink herself to death?"

"No."

"Then—"

Craig swung around. "Look, I want to have Christmas, too. I want turkey tomorrow—hell, I think even old Quintin wants turkey tomorrow. We've just got to keep things calm and him on an even keel. We can't have him going all ballistic every time he hears a noise."

"Yeah, yeah, but…what the hell is it about you that he doesn't like?" Scooter demanded, staring at him.

"Damned if I know," Craig told him, shrugging, but inside he felt sick.

I wanted to stop him from killing the old man, he thought. And maybe Quintin *hadn't* killed him. Maybe…

Quintin *had* killed him. He knew it. He had failed. God, he had failed.

He couldn't fail now. Somehow he had to find a way to disarm both men, to get them going after each other instead of the O'Boyles.

Scooter spun around. "Hey, I hear something! Over there."

Scooter started plowing his way through the snow, his gun out. Swearing softly in dismay, Craig followed.

He saw the trail leading away from the basement window through the snow and his heart sank.

Kat.

He forced his own path through the snow, somehow getting ahead of Scooter even though the other man had started off first, and then, even over the sound of the storm he heard her. Heard her desperate breath as she tried to run through the mammoth buildup of snow.

Then he heard the explosion of a bullet, followed by the soft sucking sound as it shot through the snow and into the wet ground.

"Stop!" he shouted to Scooter.

"There's someone. There *is* someone!"

Another bullet ripped through the night.

"Stop shooting!" he shouted to Scooter. "You're going to kill me."

He had to reach Kat first. He redoubled his effort, but she was young and fit.

And she was running for her life.

He ran harder, barely grimacing when his ankle caught and twisted in a rut beneath the snow.

Kat let out a gasp as another bullet exploded, far too close.

"Scooter, you idiot, stop!" Craig raged.

She was directly in front of him. He jumped for all he was worth, catching her by the shoulders. Together, they flew facedown into the snow. She screamed and fought but he was stronger than she was.

He turned her over, and shock filled her eyes when she recognized him.

"Stop fighting, please," he implored in a whisper.

"You could have let me go!"

"Don't you understand? He would have shot you. I had to take you down or else he would have killed you," he told her softly.

For a moment, she was still, eyes staring into his. Then she spat at him.

He swallowed hard. He could hear Scooter coming up behind them and knew he had to talk fast. "For the love of God, for your life, for the lives of your family, you don't know me. You've never seen me before. And quit fighting."

She stared at him. Green eyes like gems in the strange light, snow falling delicately on her cheeks. And all across the snow, the deep red flow of her hair.

Just like blood. Blood on the snow.

"Bastard!" she hissed.

He swallowed and nodded, and then Scooter was there and there was no more time to talk.

"I guess Quintin isn't such an idiot after all, huh?" Scooter demanded. "Lookee, lookee. What have we got here?" He hunkered down, grinning at Kat.

Craig didn't like the look of his grin. He liked it even less when Scooter reached out to touch her cheek.

Once again, Kat spat.

"Why you—" Scooter began. He was going to hit her.

Craig caught his hand.

Scooter stared at him, mistrust dawning in his eyes.

"No…it's Christmas, remember? Come on, Scooter, let's just make it through the night."

Apparently that made sense to Scooter, who nodded. "No more of that, girlie," he said. "Christmas or no Christmas, I *will* slug you next time." He stood. "Let's get her inside and let Quintin figure out what to do with her."

Craig nodded, trying to help Kat to her feet. She wasn't particularly cooperative.

"What the hell is going on out there?" Quintin yelled from the house.

"We got a girl!" Scooter cried out. "A wild one. The older kid's got a twin, and I think this is her."

"Tell the wild one to come along nice and quiet or Mom gets it."

Craig saw Kat's shoulders slump. Saw the utter despair and desolation darkening the emerald beauty of her eyes.

"Let's go," he said curtly.

Inwardly, he trembled and wondered how they would manage to get through the night, if there had been truth, a premonition, in that vision of her hair spread out…

Like blood on the snow.

Lionel Hudson was dead from a single bullet between the eyes.

Sheila kept feeling the sting of tears against her eyelids. Lionel had lived his years as a good man, a fair man, always ready to help others. And now he was dead.

Executed.

She raged against the idea. She didn't even feel the snow against her cheeks or the bite of the cold through her clothing.

Tim laid an arm around her shoulders. "Sheila."

"Yeah?"

"You said he had cancer."

"Yeah."

He inhaled deeply. "I've seen people die of cancer. It can be slow and painful."

She looked at him, enraged. "So this is better?"

"I'm just telling you that he's beyond pain now."

She swallowed, shaking her head. Beyond all pain.

A bitter wave of anguish seized her, and she almost laughed out loud.

"Sheila."

"Yeah?"

"Whoever did this is still out there."

She nodded, still feeling numb.

"Sheila, that other message came from just a few miles from here. Right?"

She nodded.

"I think that's where our killer is."

Again, she nodded. "We need some major help here. Like a swat team from Springfield."

"We don't have help. We have you, and we have me."

"Tim, if the man who killed Lionel—"

"I'd say it was two men. Maybe even three. The way he was dragged out here…don't think one man could have done it."

"Okay, so if these men are in the O'Boyle place… we have to be careful. They've already killed once. They'll kill again without a thought."

Tim nodded. "Maybe…" He looked away.

She frowned, her knees threatening to buckle.

"Maybe they're already dead," she said, finishing the thought he couldn't voice.

He shrugged unhappily, not meeting her eyes.

"All right. We've got to get over there as fast as we can."

"And then...?"

"We'll figure that out when we get there."

Quintin was furious, and Craig had never felt more afraid in his entire life.

When they reached the house, Quintin stared at Kat in fury, but he didn't touch her. Instead, he backhanded David with a vengeance. Skyler screamed in protest, but she'd already raced forward to grab her daughter.

The others started to move.

Oh God, this was it, Craig thought. The bullets and the blood would start now.

"Wait!" he cried, stepping forward.

But David was just as set against a bloodbath. "Stop, everyone...everyone just calm down. Please!"

"You knew she was out there!" Quintin raged, looking at David first, then swinging around to stare accusingly at the rest of the family. "You all did."

Frazier replied, his tone like ice, "We thought she was dead already. In the storm," he said flatly.

Quintin, waving his gun wildly, paced the foyer. "You know, I tried. I really tried. But you people don't learn. I'm going to have to kill one of you."

"No!" Skyler screamed.

"Come on, Quintin, if you kill anyone, we can't have Christmas," Craig said.

"Quintin," Scooter seconded quickly. "Calm down. We've got the girl. And even if we hadn't gotten her, where the hell could she have gone in this? Come on, no real harm done."

He actually smiled at Kat, as if she might be grateful. As if she might actually like him for buying time. Craig forced himself to keep still.

"You're all a pack of liars!" Quintin accused, and aimed the gun at David. "Liars."

Craig looked around, afraid someone would make a move and bring down hell. The tension in the room was palpable. "Please, Quintin," he said. "We caught the girl."

"Craig got her," Scooter said.

Quintin glanced at Craig, who stared back expressionlessly.

"Please," Skyler murmured, and walked toward Quintin. "I swear to you, Kat is our only other child. No one knows you're here. And you're an intelligent man. You can't blame us for wanting to hide her."

"And she didn't try to attack us or anything," Craig said. "She was just trying to run away."

There was silence.

Still explosive.

Tension still so thick in the air it could be cut by a knife.

If Quintin started shooting, what should he do? Craig wondered. Throw himself on the man and pray he could disarm him before getting killed, and that someone else could overpower Scooter before too many of the others died, as well?

"I need a drink," Paddy announced firmly into the silence.

"Yes," Skyler said, white as the snow, her features stretched more tightly than the wires of her piano. "Please, let's all calm down. It's late. But we...we've actually had a good day. We had a nice meal, music, a fun game. We…we have Christmas tomorrow. The snow will stop, the roads will clear, and you can escape. For now…let's have a drink."

Paddy turned and started for the kitchen.

"Hey, Mick!" Quintin thundered.

Paddy turned to him, arching a brow.

"No one goes anywhere alone."

Ignoring Quintin, the old man turned away and started walking again.

Craig caught Paddy's eyes. It was an act, he realized. The old man was terrified and playing for time.

"A drink sounds good to me, Quintin," Craig said. "I think I've still got a fever, and it was freezing out there. I need something to warm me up."

"All right. A drink," Quintin said after a long moment. "But we tie up the father first."

David's jaw tightened, but he didn't move.

"Where's there some rope in this place?" Quintin said, turning to Frazier.

"Dad, have we got any rope anywhere?"

"What kind of criminals forget rope?" Jamie muttered, sounding every inch the quintessential sulky teen.

Scooter actually laughed. Quintin cast him a venomous glare.

"You have my wife, my daughter, my sons, an innocent girl who's here as a guest and my wife's uncle. What do you think I'm going to do?" David demanded, sounding not just exhausted, but beaten.

Craig caught David O'Boyle looking at him with what seemed to be mistrust.

Well, as Scooter had said, he'd been the one to bring Kat down. That was important. Quintin had to believe in him, even if it meant that David might not.

"Everybody into the kitchen," Quintin said. "Even you, Dad. Fuck!" He swore with no apology. "There's got to be rope around here somewhere. We're not settling down for a warm winter's night until we find some rope."

Skyler didn't appear to be ready to let her daughter go, Craig noticed. She was still arm in arm with Kat as they went through the swinging door to the kitchen. "Give me this parka—it's soaked," she told her daughter.

As if a soaked parka mattered when there were men with guns in the house, he thought dryly.

But Kat slipped off the parka. "Mom, can you make me a hot toddy?"

"Yes, certainly. We don't want you catching your death of cold."

Her words hung strangely in the air.

Skyler, still white and stricken, turned to the stove. Craig watched her face as she picked up the kettle, moved the few feet to the sink and started to fill it. He could actually see her thought process. He knew she was longing to bring the water to a full boil and throw it in his face.

He decided to keep his distance.

"There was no chair for you when we got here, so I guess you weren't invited to the family dinner, huh?" Scooter asked Kat. "Why not? Were you bad?" His tone had an awkward flirty note to it that Craig found alarming.

"We miscounted," Jamie said.

"See? You miscounted, and we don't have rope. Everyone screws up," Scooter said.

"We didn't screw up," Quintin said. "We just didn't expect to be part of a group for so long."

It was a warning. They all knew it.

Quintin's mood was teetering at the edge of madness, Craig thought. The arrival of Kat O'Boyle had shaken him.

"It was cold out there. I would love a hot toddy, too, please," Craig said, to cut the tension.

The glance Skyler shot him was not forgiving.

Good God, couldn't anyone see? If he hadn't tackled her, Scooter would have killed her.

Or maybe they did see. Maybe they couldn't help but put up a wall against anyone who wasn't one of them.

"Hey, it's eleven forty-five," Scooter said. "Christmas in fifteen minutes."

"Kat…are you hurt?" Brenda asked softly.

"No, I'm fine, thanks, Brenda. Just cold."

"Brenda is great at Trivial Pursuit," Jamie said out of nowhere.

No, not out of nowhere, Craig realized. The kid was trying to diffuse the tension and get back to where they had been before Kat was discovered, when things had been calmer, easier.

"I'm not surprised. She's a straight-A student, right?" Kat said, smiling at Brenda and glancing toward her brother.

"I can't even hum 'Yankee Doodle,' though," Brenda said.

The petite little blonde was gaining in the strength department. She had looked shell-shocked for so long. Now...

She might actually be one of the calmest members of the group.

"Mrs. O'Boyle, would you mind bringing out some of those cookies you made earlier?" Brenda asked.

Quintin stepped forward. "Everyone sit."

"It's difficult to make drinks and get cookies if I'm sitting down," Skyler said.

"Don't be a wiseass," Quintin said, but the tension in him seemed to have eased down a notch. "You do the drinks."

"How about I get the cookies?" Kat suggested.

Quintin scowled at her. "You shouldn't be allowed to have any."

"But...you wouldn't expect me to be stupid, would you?" Kat asked him. "I'm sure if it had been you, you would have hidden, too."

He stared at her, then nodded. "Yeah, and I'd

have gotten away, too. Now forget the cookies and everybody sit."

They sat at the table, as ordered, and Skyler started handing out the toddies.

"Don't forget me," Jamie said.

His mother paused.

"Go ahead and give him one. Maybe he can get some sleep before…before Santa comes," David said dryly.

"Presents!" Scooter said excitedly, then looked oddly at Quintin. "Except we don't really live here."

"We always have extra presents," Skyler said.

Scooter grinned, and everyone started to drink, the tension easing into the background under an onslaught of hot whiskey.

And then the doorbell rang, and as quickly as that, the tension was back.

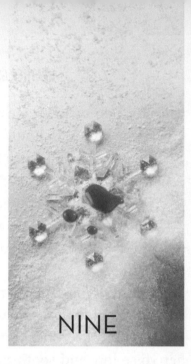

NINE

Skyler barely held back a scream.

Kat could see her mother's struggle and pleaded silently, No, Mom, no! Don't scream. It will be a bloodbath.

Quintin jumped up as if he were on springs, his gun at the ready and aimed at each of them in turn. He stared at David. "Who the hell is that?"

"I don't know," David said.

"Like you didn't know your daughter was running around outside, right?"

"I swear to God," David said quietly. "I don't know

who it is. No one else was invited over, and it's ridiculously late. We should just ignore it."

"Right. Ignore it," Craig agreed.

Quintin shook his head. "It's the cops."

"Yeah, the cops," Scooter echoed, frowning.

Quintin turned to glare accusingly at Kat. "What did you do?" he demanded.

"Nothing."

"What did you do?" he repeated.

"What could I have done?" she asked. She desperately tried to keep her eyes level with his, to keep her voice low and soothing. "Quintin, haven't you noticed? The phones are all down."

"What do you think we are?" David asked. "Magicians? This is a small town. Everyone knows we come up here for Christmas. It's probably just someone wanting to make sure we weathered the storm all right."

"I'm telling you, it's the cops," Quintin said, still looking at Kat.

"If it is, they're probably just checking on all the houses they can reach," Kat said, staring back at Quintin with complete innocence. "The office is just a few miles down the road. They'll have seen our lights." Her heart was racing. What if the officers barged in, saying they'd gotten her message? What if they walked in with their guns cocked?

The bell rang again, ratcheting up the tension. She swallowed, turning slightly and praying she wouldn't give herself away. Because they were right. It had to be the cops at the door. And when they came in...

She looked over at her mother, knowing that any call from this address was already suspect, thanks to Jamie and that prank he'd pulled.

Which was going to be worse? Cops thinking they were pulling another prank and coming in unprepared, or taking it seriously and walking in ready to shoot?

Maybe neither. Maybe there was a God.

There had to be a way to tell them they were under siege.

Quintin pointed at Skyler. "You. Over here by me. Scooter, you and Craig take the family and answer the door. Except for you, kid." He pointed at Jamie. "You stay in here, too. The rest of you, greet them and get rid of them. If you don't, I'll kill your mom and your brother. And if you cause any trouble out there, the cops will die, too."

"It might not be the cops," Frazier said.

"Yeah? Well, whoever it is, get rid of them."

The bell rang for a third time, and Quintin looked even edgier than before.

"Scooter…you and Craig can be brothers. Craig… you're the daughter's boyfriend. I'm warning you all, my finger's twitching. I'm going to be sorry if Mom here doesn't make it to Christmas, but I swear, I *will* kill her *and* the boy if anyone makes a wrong move out there. Do you all understand?" Quintin demanded.

"They'll break the door down if they have to ring that bell any longer," Craig pointed out quietly.

"Go!" Quintin ordered.

David led the family out to the foyer to answer the door. Kat followed, aware that Craig was right behind her, painfully aware that Quintin was holding Jamie and her mother at gunpoint in the kitchen.

As Kat watched, her father looked out the peephole. Her entire throat felt constricted. She prayed that the police wouldn't come barging in, demanding to know who had sent out a plea for help.

Maybe it hadn't gotten through and this really was just a courtesy call because of the storm.

"Well?" Scooter demanded from behind Brenda, who was gripping Frazier's hand tightly.

"It *is* the cops," David said.

"Open the door. And no tricks. If you betray me, your wife dies, your kid dies, and I'll take down your daughter first, you got it?" Scooter said.

David reached for the door.

"And quit looking like scared rabbits, all of you!" Scooter demanded. "Act naturally."

David nodded and opened the door.

There were two of them outside. They were in their county uniforms, under deep blue, heavy, hooded coats, and they were wearing clunky boots because of the snow. Kat knew the woman, Sergeant Sheila Polanski. She'd first met her when she'd been a very young child. The young man—tall, fit, friendly looking, not really handsome but with a nice smile—was a stranger.

Don't say anything about a text message, she begged in silence. Don't even look at us curiously, please.

To her amazement, they were both smiling. Shivering, but smiling.

Maybe her text really hadn't gotten through.

"Sheila, my God, how are you?" David said. "What are you doing out here on Christmas Eve?"

"Just checking that everyone's okay. Mind if we come in?" Sheila asked, stepping forward without waiting for an answer or an invitation.

With no other option, David led their two visitors into the living room. "David, this is Tim Graystone. He just started working with us a few months back."

"How do you do," Tim said, shaking David's hand.

"Tim," Sheila said, casually sweeping out a hand, "this is Frazier O'Boyle, his twin, Kat, their great-uncle, Patrick—and how are you, Paddy, you old coot?" she demanded.

"Fine, me darlin', fine," Paddy said, giving Sheila a hug.

"How's the hip?"

"Healin' fine, lass, healin' just fine," Paddy replied.

"And let's see," Sheila continued. "I'm sorry, David. I can't introduce your guests, because I can't say that I know them."

"Sheila, Tim, I'd like you to meet my son's girl-friend, Brenda, and this is…Craig," David said.

Craig slipped an arm around Kat, and it was all she

could do not to jump clear out of her skin. She managed to keep her smile in place.

"I'm with Kat," Craig said, then nodded in Scooter's direction. "This is my brother. We call him Scooter."

"A big Christmas welcome to you all," Sheila said.

"So, Sheila, what's it like out there? Storm letting up? Everyone okay?"

Kat was amazed that her father managed to speak so casually, but then, she was equally amazed she could stand there herself, smiling as if nothing were wrong, while all the time pure panic was racing helter-skelter through her veins.

"Power's down everywhere," Sheila told him.

"So we decided we'd just check in on people, make sure no one is freezing or sick and can't get to a hospital," Tim said.

He seemed like a nice guy, Kat thought, and prayed that he wouldn't die tonight. He'd sounded so convincing, too. Could it be true that they really had just happened by?

"Where's the missus?" Sheila asked David.

"Skyler? Oh, she tired out a while ago. She's in bed," David said.

"Well, since I doubt I'll see her tomorrow, you give her my Christmas regards," Sheila said.

"Sure thing."

"What about your youngest?" Sheila asked.

"Jamie? He went to bed a while ago, too."

"A teenager in bed?" Sheila said skeptically, but she was grinning.

"He believes in Santa," Kat joked quickly, just in case Sheila was going to push the issue.

"A teenager who still believes in Santa?" Tim asked politely.

Craig squeezed Kat a little too tightly to him and said, "No, what Jamie actually believes in is the prospect of presents."

"Yeah," David said. "He knows there's a new computer under the tree for him. He was ready as hell to go to bed so he can get up and claim it at the crack of dawn."

"Waking us all up with him," Frazier groaned.

"We can't sleep late?" Craig asked Kat.

She forced herself to look up with a lover's smile—something she found it all too easy to do. "No, darling, I'm afraid we can't. It's Christmas."

"Ah, young love," Paddy murmured. "Much like what we share, Sheila, me love."

Sheila just laughed, shaking her head.

"I've half a mind to move up here full-time and make an honest woman of ye," Paddy said to her.

Sheila looked from Scooter to Craig, shaking her head. "He's quite the character, isn't he?" She smiled.

"You two don't look much alike," Tim said thoughtfully, inclining his head from Craig to Scooter.

"We're half brothers," Craig said.

Everything seemed to be going okay, Kat thought, wondering what she could possibly have expected when she sent that text. Quintin had Jamie and her mother hostage, and with Scooter and Craig hovering, there was no way to get information to Sheila and Tim. Now all she wanted was for them to say goodbye and get out, to save themselves.

"I hate to intrude, but…have you got some coffee going by any chance?" Tim asked. "It's freezing out there, and we could really stand to warm up."

Kat prayed that the silence that seemed to last an eon was really only a few seconds. "Coffee?" she breathed.

"Have a seat. I'll throw on a pot," David said.

"Tim," Sheila chastised. "We can't inconvenience the O'Boyles like that."

"It's no problem," Kat said. "I'll put the coffee on, Dad." She extricated herself from Craig's arm. "Be right back."

"Please," Craig said softly.

Please…what? she wondered, and knew, as she headed toward the kitchen, that he was watching her go.

In her mind, she could see the look in his eyes, see him looking at her as he had once done. What was it? Why was he here? Had he really saved her from being shot? Was he the world's best actor? And if he was, who was he playing, her family—or his supposed cohorts?

She pushed open the door to the kitchen, terrified of what she might find. Jamie and her mother were sitting side by side at the table, Quintin standing behind her mother with the nose of his gun pressed against her temple.

Kat's heart lurched. His finger did indeed look to be twitching, just as he'd said.

"It's going fine," she said softly to him. "The young cop just wants a cup of coffee."

Quintin frowned fiercely. Kat watched his trigger finger, almost afraid to swallow.

"Look, they think Mom and Jamie are in bed. They'll be gone as soon as they get their coffee. It will be fine," she whispered quickly.

The gun moved away from her mother's head for a moment as he indicated the counter. "Do it."

Skyler stared at her daughter, her hazel eyes wide but steady.

Kat turned and quickly prepared the coffee, then reached under the counter.

"What the hell are you doing?" Quintin demanded in a heated growl.

"Getting a tray. For cups, and cream and sugar," Kat said, noticing that her mother and Jamie had both hands on the table. As she watched, Skyler took her son's hand and gently squeezed it.

The swinging door opened slightly. "Sweetheart," Craig said, "how's that coffee coming?"

"Almost ready," she said, thanking God that her mother had one of the new pots that made a full pot in sixty seconds.

"I'll take a cup, too, babe," he said.

"Anyone else?" she asked.

"Yeah, your dad."

The exchange sounded so casual, so easy, she thought. "Okay. It's coming."

"Do you need help?"

"No, thanks. I'll be right out."

She tried not to shake as she got the creamer and the sugar bowl and set them on the tray. She could feel Quintin's eyes on her as she poured four cups of coffee. Done, she turned to look at him again.

The gun was once again pressed against her mother's temple.

Skyler managed to smile at her, then Kat hurried out, her back pushing against the swinging door to open it. She had barely reached the living room before Craig was there to take the tray from her. His eyes met hers, and for a moment, she dared to believe.

But...

Even if he was on their side, what could he do? He didn't have a gun, which meant Quintin would shoot at least one of them before he could be stopped.

Craig set the tray on the coffee table. Brenda was

cuddled up on Frazier's lap in one of the big arm-chairs. Her father was seated in the other, while Uncle Paddy had chosen the love seat. He was rolling his cane between his hands, and when his eyes touched hers, they were grave. Then Sheila spoke to him, and he quickly laughed. The show was on, she thought.

Tim and Sheila were on the sofa. Scooter was standing by the fireplace, one elbow resting on the mantel. She could see the bulge of his gun tucked into his waistband beneath his flannel shirt.

Couldn't the cops see it, too?

But Sheila wasn't even looking at Scooter. "I've been telling Tim how talented all you kids are," she said. "Would you play something for him, Kat?"

Kat saw that Craig had taken a seat beside Sheila on the sofa. He seemed very calm. Of course he was. He was one of *them*, after all. Or was he? And what the hell was going on in the kitchen now? Was Quintin hearing this? How could she possibly play the piano? Why didn't Craig or Scooter say something to stop this farce?

"My mom is the one who can really play," Kat said.

"You're good, too, Kat. How about just one song while we finish our coffee?" Sheila suggested.

Frazier lifted Brenda off his lap and joined Kat at the piano. "Let's do our public servants a Christmas Eve kindness and give them some music with their coffee," he said. "I'll sing backup."

"No, you sing lead, and I'll take the harmony," Kat said.

"Sure."

Her twin's eyes met hers, and she knew that he was trying to look reassuring, strong. As if help were an actual possibility.

She stared back at him, her smile sad. They both knew that Quintin and the others were counting on them to play it out until the end, and that they were all going to die.

But we'll pretend until the bitter end, she thought, and looked around the room as she started to play.

Scooter looked almost misty-eyed, as he stared at them from his place by the mantel. Her father's fingers were clenching the arms of his chair. Craig was leaning toward Sheila, looking as if he'd just finished saying something. And Sheila…

Sheila didn't seem to be paying any attention to

the music. She was watching Scooter with a thoughtful look on her face, as if she were weighing whatever Craig had just said.

Despite herself, Kat felt hope begin to bloom in her heart.

She turned back to the piano, and she and Frazier launched into a song. When they finished, their audience broke into applause. Tim even gave them a standing ovation. "Sheila, you were right. They're great."

"Thanks very much," Frazier said, then walked back to rejoin Brenda in the armchair.

"Well, I guess we'd better be going back out into the cold," Sheila said with a sigh. She and Tim both rose and started toward the door.

Craig walked casually over to Kat and slipped an arm around her waist. She swallowed. She couldn't pull away without revealing the pretense behind their relationship, much less turn on him and demand to know the truth.

For the moment she needed to focus on being grateful that he could play his part so well. She needed to thank God that her text message, which had once seemed to be their only hope, hadn't gone through. She needed to just keep playing her part so Sheila and Tim would leave.

Before they all wound up dead.

Craig led her to the door, where everyone was congregating to say goodbye.

"Have you checked on the other families in the area?" Frazier asked.

Was there a slight hesitation before they answered? Kat wondered. A moment when the two officers looked at each other almost conspiratorially?

"We checked in on everyone we could get to. I was a bit worried about Mrs. Auffen—she's eighty, you know. But she was fine. Everyone in this area has a generator," Sheila said.

"I've trying to convince Sheila that we can go back to the office and warm up while we wait for the morning crew," Tim said.

"If they make it in," Sheila said skeptically. "I have a feeling we'll be on till afternoon," she said to Tim, who just shrugged.

"Well, good night, folks. And thanks for the coffee, and the entertainment," Sheila said.

"Yeah, thank you, guys," Tim said. "It was nice to meet you."

"Good night. Take care," David said.

"Drive safe," Craig added.

The two cops were almost out the door. Any second they would be in the clear, Kat thought, and she could rush back into the kitchen and see if her mother was all right.

"Hey, wait," Scooter said suddenly, his voice low, sounding like a growl deep in his throat.

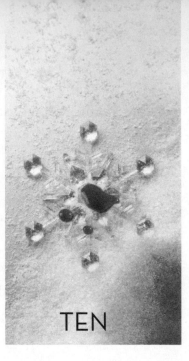

TEN

Craig's heart froze in his chest. They were in the clear, dammit. The cops were leaving. And they knew. *They knew.* He'd managed to whisper a few words to Sergeant Polanski, and she had nodded her understanding. They were safe, at least for now, and the cops would come back when they could do something. It was a miracle.

Or so it had seemed. But now…just when they were leaving, Scooter was stopping them. What the hell was going on?

"Wait," Scooter repeated.

"What?" Craig asked, knowing he must sound almost desperate, as he stared at Scooter.

"We're forgetting something," Scooter explained. His narrow face seemed to broaden with his sudden smile. "It's Christmas!" Scooter exclaimed. "It's Christmas Day. Merry Christmas!"

Craig thought his sigh of relief was almost as loud as the blizzard that was still raging, although with a little less vehemence than before, just outside the open door.

But Scooter was still grinning, apparently unaware of anything besides his own joy in the holiday. "Come on, everybody. Wish each other Merry Christmas."

"Right. Merry Christmas," David gasped in what was clearly relief.

"Merry Christmas, Bren," Frazier said, then smiled down at his tiny girlfriend and lightly kissed her lips.

"Merry Christmas, Dad," Kat said, and turned to her father.

Of course, Craig told himself, trying to tamp down what he knew was an irrational sense of disappointment.

"Sheila, me love." Paddy laughed, and hugged the deputy.

"Merry Christmas, bro," Scooter said, and shot Craig a warning look before hugging him.

Brother? Craig thought. Oh, no. Not in any way. But he couldn't allow himself to show his revulsion—his horror at how this night was turning out.

He'd known all along that Quintin and Scooter were thieves, he just hadn't realized how much could be stolen. Not just property, but sanity. Love. Christmas spirit.

Lives.

He drew away from Scooter, trying to maintain a cheerful expression as he watched the others. They had gone from Christmas Eve to Christmas Day, a time to offer love and the olive branch of peace to family and friends.

Under Scooter's encouraging eye, Kat gave her brother a hug. Then Paddy and Brenda and even Tim and Sheila.

And then him.

He tried. He tried so hard with his eyes, to explain everything he had never been able to tell her. To somehow make her understand that he'd never intended to be here tonight, to bring danger to her family's door. That he hadn't shared the truth before because the truth had been too painful, and because, at the time, he'd believed that even if she knew the truth, she couldn't—wouldn't—love him.

He lifted her chin and said softly, "Merry Christmas, Kat. And many, many more," he added, even more softly, then lightly kissed her lips.

And she didn't pull away.

She stared hard at him when he finally lifted his head. She'd always had the most beautiful eyes. Irish eyes, green cat eyes to fit her name.

Sheila cleared her throat. "We'd really better go. The best to you all. Good night."

"Merry Christmas," Tim said.

And then, finally, the door closed behind them, and Craig was able to let out a silent sigh of relief at last. The cops were gone. It was Christmas Day. And he'd already witnessed a miracle.

No one here had died, and finally they had hope.

* * *

"They're gone," Craig announced, pushing his way through the swinging door. "They're gone, Quintin, and the O'Boyles played it just like pros."

The sound of the opening door had made Skyler jump. Actually, any movement made her jump. And that wasn't particularly smart, because every time she started, she felt the touch of the gun. One of these times she would startle Quintin, and without even thinking, he would pull the trigger.

"I probably should have killed them," Quintin said thoughtfully, almost as if he weren't still standing behind her, his words casual—as if he didn't still have a gun pressed against her temple.

"Quintin, no," Craig argued. "You don't want to kill cops. It makes other cops crazy. They've been here, and now they're gone, and they're not suspicious of anything. Think about it. It's the best thing that could have happened."

"Yeah, maybe," Quintin said, but there was no conviction in his voice.

Skyler didn't like the other man's tone. He sounded more on edge than ever.

"Quintin, I'm telling you the truth," Craig said.

Skyler didn't like the curl of Quintin's lips. The man was sneering. Quintin didn't like Craig, really didn't like Craig. And Quintin was the one who called the shots.

While Craig…

Scooter had boasted that the man had been the one to catch Kat. Maybe so, but just looking at him, and then at Kat, she was certain there was more to the story. Something was going on between the two of them. It was as if they knew each other. Certainly they were close enough in age for it to be a possibility, but Frazier didn't seem to know him.

And what the hell difference did it make whether he and Kat knew each other or not?

A lot. Because things might come to a point when the only thing that mattered was whether Craig was with them…or against them.

Scooter came barging through the swinging door, herding the rest of the family in front of them. "It's Christmas," he said happily. "Merry Christmas, Quintin!"

"Merry Christmas, Scooter," Quintin said, but he

didn't move. At Skyler's side, neither did Jamie. It felt as if a week had gone by, as if the three of them had been frozen there forever.

She squeezed her son's hand. *Giving false encouragement?* she taunted herself. But maybe it wasn't false.

And wasn't it a parent's job to teach hope against all odds?

She dared to turn her head away from the muzzle of the gun and face her son. "Well, we made it through another crisis," she said, and forced a smile. She released his hand and looked up at Quintin. "May I turn the coffeepot off?"

"Yeah, go ahead."

She rose, and David ignored their captors and strode straight over to her, then slipped his arms around her, turning her to face him. She frowned slightly, wondering how the cops had come and gone without noticing that both Frazier and David had darkening bruises on their faces.

"Merry Christmas, Skyler," David said, and he kissed her.

She kissed him back, forgetting for a few seconds

that they had an audience and pouring all her love for him and her relief that they had made it this far and were still alive into the kiss.

"Get a room," Frazier teased.

"We have a room," David said, grinning slightly and not looking away from his wife.

"Yeah, they have a room, they're just not going to be using it tonight," Quintin said.

"But would it be okay to get some sleep?" Jamie asked.

"Sure. Anyone who wants to can drift off right in the living room," Quintin said.

"I could never sleep," Skyler said with conviction.

"How about you just try to rest?" David suggested.

"You'd better rest. You have to cook that turkey in the morning," Scooter said.

Skyler nodded, suddenly exhausted. "All right, I'll try."

"Not until I've had me chance to say Merry Christmas to me niece," Paddy announced. He walked over to her and hugged her, taking the chance to whisper, "Sheila knows."

She hugged him more tightly, adrenaline racing

through her. Was he crazy? Was he just trying to give her hope?

Or could it be true?

As Paddy pulled away, she lowered her eyes to hide the light of hope, choosing to believe what he'd said was true—that the cops knew—and realizing that everything had to be played out meticulously.

Or else someone would die.

Sheila didn't want to go far from the O'Boyle house, but it was freezing and the snow was still flying and their snowmobiles didn't offer any protection against the storm. She also knew they had to carefully weigh every possible course of action and that they wouldn't think clearly if they were freezing.

Her small Colonial house was closer to the O'Boyle residence than the office was, so she led the way there to make plans. Since they had no way of communicating to anyone from the office, anyway, it didn't make much sense to go all that way back.

"I know that guy's face," Tim told Sheila, rubbing his hands in front of the fire she had quickly stoked. "The youngest one."

"From where?"

"I don't know. But I've seen him."

Sheila was doubtful. "On a most-wanted list?" she asked skeptically. "I sure don't know who he is. That's not the kind of face you forget. But he managed to talk to me. Smooth as silk. He told me there were two armed men, the one we saw and another one in the kitchen with Mrs. O'Boyle and Jamie, and he'd kill them if we acted suspicious in any way. He said we had to find a way to take them both down."

Tim glanced at her. "He said all that?"

"Right in the middle of an Irish lullaby," she said flatly.

"Well, we thought our guys might be in there," he said.

She produced a piece of paper. "He was definitely telling the truth. Paddy Murphy slipped this into my pocket."

Tim took the note from her. It was crumpled, since Paddy had wadded it into a tiny ball before slipping it into her pocket when he hugged her.

"'Two men with guns. Must be taken together.

Will kill if threatened. Be careful,'" Tim read aloud. He looked at her. "Clever old geezer," he said.

"Thank God we went in carefully," she said. "But what do we do? Try to get hold of the state police somehow? If we go at them with enough guns…"

"No," Tim said.

She looked at him.

"Sheila, Lionel Hudson is already dead. They killed him. It won't make any difference to them if they have to kill again. If we go up against them in force, the first thing they'll do is kill that family just to get them out of the way."

They were both silent, thinking.

"He had it right, that guy Craig," Sheila said. "Scooter, or whatever his real name is, and the guy in the kitchen have to be taken down together."

"The question is, how?" Tim said, turning away from the fire to pace. "We can come up with some excuse and go back over there."

"Sure. And then we're up against the same thing we were before, only this time we know it. One of them will hole up somewhere with a couple of the O'Boyles, and he'll kill them if we make a move.

They'll do it—even if they're going to die themselves—because they don't intend to go down alone."

"Oh God," Tim said suddenly.

"What?"

"They're going to figure out pretty soon that not
only have we figured out who they are, but that
we've seen their faces. If they want to get away clean,
they'll need to kill us, too."

"Tim, we have to go at this logically and reasonably," Sheila said.

"What about negotiations, then?" he asked.

"They won't negotiate, I'm sure of it," Sheila said.
"But we won't give in, either. And we'll have help,"
Sheila said.

He looked at her questioningly.

"The family," she said. "They're not armed, and
they're scared as hell, but I promise you, they'll fight
to the death for one another."

He nodded. "Good point."

"And I don't know who the hell that Craig kid is,
but he'll help us, too. He's not one of them."

"Maybe he was just trying to sucker you in,"
Tim warned.

"No, he was being honest. I'd swear to it," Sheila said.

"Here's the thing. I'm armed, you're armed, and the killers are armed. There's not going to be a chance for any warning shots. We have to take them both out."

"Easier said than done," Sheila replied.

"We just have to get back in that house."

"Ring the doorbell again?" Sheila said. "I don't think so."

"Of course not. We have to get in without being seen."

The house remained comfortably warm, despite the bitter cold outside. Thanks to the generator, the lights on the tree continued to blink their message of Christmas cheer. But the living room was silent.

Quintin had dragged one of the big upholstered chairs over to block the front door and was on guard, a watchful eye on the living room, his gun resting comfortably in his lap. Scooter was in the other armchair, asleep, his gun tucked in his waistband, where no one could steal it without waking him.

Uncle Paddy had the love seat, Kat's parents were

on the couch, and everyone else had blankets right on the floor. Kat was all too aware of Craig lying right up against her, even though there was no longer any need to keep up the pretense of being a couple.

Time ticked by. Kat watched the clock. Nearly one o'clock.

One-thirty.

She had to believe in a miracle. Had to believe that what Uncle Paddy had whispered to her under cover of a good-night hug was true—Sheila and Tim would be back, and would have the good sense not to come in with guns blazing. Because if they did?

Quintin would take out half her family before he died.

Her mother was curled against her father, and Mom's eyes were actually closed. If she could ignore the circumstances, they made a nice picture. She so seldom saw them this comfortable with each other anymore.

She shifted, trying to get more comfortable, and Quintin's hand tightened on his gun. He eyed her for a long time without saying anything, so she closed her eyes and pretended to rest.

A moment later, she barely withheld a scream when Craig threw an arm across her in his sleep and pulled her closer. She gritted her teeth, ready to push him away, and then she realized that he wasn't asleep at all. His eyes were open, and he was staring at her intently, meaningfully. "Keep it together," he whispered. "They're coming back. And they know what's going on."

Her eyes widened. "How do you know that?"

"I told them."

She was silent for a very long time. "I wish I believed you."

For a second, he wore a pained expression. "I wish you did, too," he said. And then it was as if something fell over his eyes. A curtain. As if…

As if he wouldn't allow himself to care.

"Quiet down, all of you!" Scooter snapped, waking up suddenly, apparently under the impression that something was going on.

He must have been dreaming, Kat thought, and looked at the clock.

Two o'clock.

She couldn't believe it, but despite her fear and the

disconcerting presence of Craig beside her, her eye-lids were starting to droop. She was exhausted.

Her mother and father appeared to be sleeping. Frazier's eyes were closed. Jamie hadn't moved.

She looked across the room. Uncle Paddy's eyes were only half closed. His lips twitched, and he gave her a thumbs-up sign.

She tried to smile in return.

In the end, after going over and over the possibilities, Sheila and Tim decided that trying to slip into the house in the middle of the night would be a mistake.

It seemed most likely—though not, they thought with grave concern, certain—that if it came to a massacre, it wouldn't be until night fell on Christmas Day. Sheila had lived in the area her whole life, and she could second-guess the wind and read the snowfall. This storm wasn't going to slack off enough to allow the killers to escape for hours, at least.

With his military training, Tim was the expert in subterfuge, and in his opinion, given that there were only two of them, trying to enter the house in the dead of night, when at least one of the killers would be alert and on guard but the family would most likely be asleep and too disoriented to help in their own rescue, would be a grave mistake.

They decided to make their move just before daybreak. They would take the snowmobiles as far as they could without risking being heard, then walk the rest of the way. Their plan was to reach the house with darkness as a cover, but not to attempt a break-in until the inhabitants were actually rising.

"I think we're crazy," Sheila said.

"No, you think *I'm* crazy," Tim said with a smile.

"Whatever," Sheila said dryly.

"Are you ready?" he asked.

"Hell, no. So let's go over it one more time."

Tim frowned. "I just wish I could remember where I've seen that Craig guy before." He paused in concentration. "Maybe not actually him…maybe just a picture of him."

"And you're absolutely certain it wasn't the ten-most-wanted list?"

Tim shook his head. "I'm certain. Anyway, you said the guy is trying to help us."

"Yeah."

"But what if…?"

"What if it's all a lie? What if he's trying to trick us?" Sheila asked him.

Tim didn't answer.

Kat couldn't remember how the hours had passed, or just what time it was when she finally drifted off.

When she awoke, she was wrapped in Craig's arms. And he wasn't sleeping anymore, either.

His fingers were gently stroking her hair. She turned and caught his eyes, and for a second she froze, just watching him. There was so much pain in his gaze.

Then a shield slipped over his gaze and he shifted uncomfortably. "Sorry," he murmured.

Was that for the sake of Quintin and Scooter? Because she had the impression he wasn't really sorry at all, that for a moment he had been living in the past, remembering a time when they had so often fallen asleep together, then woken up in each other's arms.

She closed her eyes in anguish. For just a moment, she had been living in the past, as well.

It was coming up on first light, she realized, the

darkness not as thick as it had been. Everyone else was waking up, too, she saw.

"I see people are finally up," Quintin said. "Good. Because I'd like some coffee."

"Coffee, sure," Skyler said.

"I'll make it, Mom," Kat said, getting to her feet.

And away from Craig.

She stretched, one eye on Quintin, who looked wide-awake. She wondered if he'd stayed up all night.

"Scooter, you awake?" Quintin asked.

"Yeah."

"Good. You keep an eye on the happy family, and I'll go watch our little escape artist make the coffee."

"Wait," Skyler said.

Quintin turned to look at her.

"Bathroom break," Skyler said, "And don't tell me you're coming in with me, because you'll have to shoot me right now."

"That can be arranged," Quintin said, his eyes narrowed dangerously.

"Hey," David snapped. "Just do what you did last night. Let everyone have a minute's privacy. It's not like we don't all need the same thing."

Quintin didn't look happy, Kat thought, but he must have decided that the alternative was worse, because he let everyone line up and take a turn in the downstairs bathroom. As for him, he must have a bladder the size of a football, she thought. He hadn't gone all night, and it didn't seem that he had to go now.

Or maybe…

Maybe his faith in Scooter was so small that he didn't dare disappear, even for a moment.

"You. Make the coffee and get something on for breakfast," he said to Skyler.

"Don't talk to my wife that way," David said, then added, "Please."

"All right. Please, Mrs. O'Boyle, coffee and breakfast."

"Since you asked so nicely…" Skyler murmured sarcastically.

"I'll help my mother," Jamie offered.

"I can set the table," Brenda said.

"Sure. Scooter. You watch them. Craig, you get in here, too. You," he said, pointing a finger at Kat. "Come with me."

"Wait a minute," her father said, frowning.

"Calm down, Dad," Quintin said. "I just want to ask the girl a few questions, that's all."

"Where are you going with her?"

"I just want to open the door and see the weather," Quintin said.

Frazier spoke up warily. "I can give you a weather report. The weather sucks."

"The snow's not going to stop until tonight," Paddy said. Quintin looked at him skeptically. "I can tell, man. I can feel it in me hip. The weather won't be letting up for hours, till darkness, I say."

Quintin gave him a strange look. Kat wondered if he knew they were all aware they would only live as long as the roads were impassable.

As soon as everyone else had gone into the kitchen, Quintin turned to Kat. "Open the front door," he told her, gesturing with his gun.

She shrugged and walked ahead of him across the foyer and did as he'd commanded.

The snow was still coming down, but the house had gotten so warm that the blast of cold air actually felt good for a moment.

"Step outside," Quintin told her.

Swallowing hard, all too aware that he was standing behind her, a gun to her back, did so.

"Turn around."

Did he mean to shoot her in the face, so she could see death coming?

Slowly, she turned around, her mind racing.

"Who is Craig?" he demanded, following her out into the snow and closing the door behind him.

"What?" she gasped, astonished.

"You know him," he said.

"I know he's a filthy bastard who's broken into my house and threatened my family," she said.

She was stunned when he lashed out, striking her hard across the cheek. "I want the truth," he announced.

"I just said—"

"The truth. Or I'll knock your front teeth out next," he said.

He couldn't let it happen, Craig thought. If Quintin had Kat outside, he wanted something, and he would hurt her to get it.

He tried to act nonchalant in front of the family and Scooter, but he knew her parents and the rest of her family were going just as insane as he was, knowing she was outside with Quintin.

David broke first and started toward the kitchen door.

"Get back here!" Scooter shouted. "Don't make me shoot you."

"Everybody calm down," Craig said. "Stay cool. I'll go out and see what's going on, okay?"

"Craig," Scooter said with a frown. "Didn't Quintin say—"

"Yeah, but you don't want to have a riot before the turkey, right?" he demanded.

He didn't wait for Scooter to answer. He turned around and headed out, praying that Scooter wouldn't do something stupid.

The minute he opened the front door, he saw that Kat's cheek was bright red. That bastard had hit her! It was all he could do not to behave like a suicidal idiot and attack Quintin right then and there.

"What's going on?" he asked as casually as he could.

"I didn't ask you to come out here," Quintin said.

"I thought you'd want to know her dad is getting antsy and I'm worried that he's going to do something stupid."

Quintin stared at him, then sneered and shrugged. "I was just telling Miss O'Boyle here that she needed to tell me where she knows you from. Now. Before I take out her teeth."

Craig's jaw nearly dropped.

"But now that you're here, you can tell me. Or I *will* shove her teeth down her throat. Maybe break her nose in the process."

Craig stared at him as incredulously as he could. "What the hell are you talking about?" he asked.

Quintin had turned to face him, momentarily taking his attention off Kat, and Craig was suddenly glad as hell, because he could see something behind one of the snowbanks.

Something blue.

Cop blue. Sheriff's-department blue.

"Quit screwing around. I'll shoot you faster than you can exhale if you cross me," Quintin said.

Craig dared to hesitate before responding. The snowbanks didn't provide much cover, and whoever was out there was trying to get around to the back of the house. He had to keep Quintin's attention on him until their rescuer was safely out of sight. "We knew each other in school," he finally said, figuring the truth—or at least a piece of it—was the best defense.

"Ages ago," Kat said.

"We went to the same college, Quintin, and that's that," he said.

Thankfully, Quintin was still staring at him, frowning. "College?"

"College," Kat repeated firmly.

"You've got a college degree, pretty boy?" Quintin demanded. "You telling me that's where Scooter found you? Like I'd believe that."

"He doesn't have a degree. He dropped out," Kat said.

"But you knew each other there," Quintin said, his skepticism clear in his tone.

"We just told you that," Craig said. The cops were safely out of sight. Of course, if Quintin went for a walk right now, he would see the prints in the snow, but there was no reason for Quintin to go for a walk.

He had to play it cool, but he also had to get Quintin back in the house and give the cops time to find the door or window or whatever it was that Kat had used to slip out last night. Then they could hide in the house, listening, until the right time came for them to make their move.

"Who else do you know in there?" Quintin demanded.

"No one," Craig said.

"Never met her folks?"

"Why would I have met them?" Craig asked impatiently.

"She never brought you home?"

"We had a few classes together. We didn't date," Kat said, staring straight at Quintin.

"We need to go back in," Craig said. "I'm worried about what Scooter might do if her parents start freaking."

"Fine. But remember this. I'm not interested in women and true love. If you cause trouble, I'll kill you. If you try to stand up for this broad, Craig, I'll kill you. Got it?"

How he longed to put his fist through Quintin's face.

"I haven't caused any trouble," Kat said.

"Oh, yeah?" Quintin squinted, assessing her long and hard. "No trouble? What do you call trying to escape last night?" He stared at her assessingly for a long time, then at Craig, and finally at the sky.

"Quintin," Craig said, trying not to let the edge of fear snaking through him show in the tone of his voice. "Quintin, what are you doing? Come on. Don't rile everyone up by making them think…by making them worry about something that isn't even happening. Let's go back in. Before Scooter does something stupid."

"Please?" Kat said.

"Right," Quintin said at last. "It's Christmas Day. Time to make the turkey, huh?"

"My mother will make a great breakfast first," Kat said. She was losing it. Craig could hear it in her voice. "If we get in there now!"

"You don't call the shots, little girl. But…" Quintin paused, let the silence draw out menacingly, then smiled. "By all means, let's go in." He swept out an arm, and she walked into the house first, followed by Craig.

And then by Quintin.

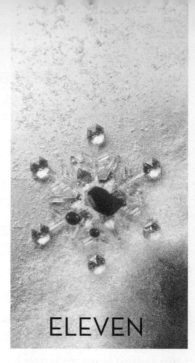

ELEVEN

Skyler thought it was amazing she hadn't burned the bacon into charcoal or ruined the French toast. She had never felt such terror. Blood, bone, muscle…her entire system was flooded with it, and she was shaking so badly she could barely stand. But she had to keep moving.

That monster had taken her daughter.

She was afraid David would explode. Frazier looked like a powder key ready to blow. Even Jamie looked as if he was going to go through the roof.

Only Paddy was managing to remain calm.

"David, pour the coffee and bring me a cup, will ye? Me legs botherin' me more than a mite."

David tried. He poured the coffee. But, glancing his way, Skyler was afraid that one of the cups was going to shatter in his hands.

"Skyler, lass, that smells good enough to tempt the fairies, so it does," Paddy said. "Now, turkey, turkey is a fine meal. But I'm as happy meself with the likes of your French toast, though why they call it *French* toast makes no sense to me, no sense at all."

"I have no idea, Uncle Paddy," Skyler replied, wondering how on earth he could sound so calm and what he was up to.

"Who knows and who cares?" Frazier said, his eyes on his father.

Skyler was afraid that the glances being exchanged between father and son indicated that they were ready to attempt another go against Scooter. She had to find a way to stop them before they invited disaster.

Scooter was perched on one of the stools at the counter, his gun out, the safety off. She knew David and Frazier were both willing to die for Kat, but she didn't want that to happen, and if they moved now, it almost certainly would.

And then Kat, out there with Quintin, would certainly die, as well.

What about Craig? she wondered. Were his cohorts planning on killing him, too, when they didn't need him anymore?

But just when she thought hope was gone, Kat came striding into the kitchen, Craig and Quintin behind her.

"Smells good in here," Quintin said pleasantly, as if he weren't still holding a gun.

She couldn't quite manage a thanks, not at that moment. "It's the bacon and coffee, I imagine."

"I'll take a coffee," Quintin said.

"I'll get it," Craig offered quickly. As he poured, he smiled at Skyler.

"What the hell?" Quintin growled. "You said you never met her before."

"And I haven't. Can't a man smile at a pretty woman? What the hell is your problem, Quintin?" Craig demanded.

"Have *you* ever met him before?" Quintin said to David.

"Where the hell would I have met him?"

"You?" Quintin spun around to stare at Frazier, who shook his head.

"Oh, for the love of God," Craig said to Quintin. "I went to the same college as Kat. We had a few classes together." He turned to the others. "Now Quintin here thinks I'm conspiring with you. That I managed to wreck the car in front of your house." He turned back to Quintin and eyed the other man challengingly. "Damned difficult, since *I was knocked out* when it happened," he said, glaring.

"You went to college with Kat?" Skyler said, ignoring the last part of his speech.

"Yes," he said, then, eager to change the subject to something less fraught with pitfalls, asked, "Hey, is that French toast?"

"It is, and if you want to get that serving platter, the first batch is ready to go," Skyler said.

"Forget that," Quintin said as Craig reached for the platter. "Where's my damn coffee?"

"Hell, you distracted me," Craig told him.

"I'll get the coffee," Brenda chirped, rising and picking up the cup Craig had left on the counter.

"You!" Quintin said suddenly, pointing at her. "Did you ever see this guy before?"

Brenda handed him the coffee, which he took with his left hand, his right still brandishing the gun.

"I told you, I'm pre-med," Brenda said. "Not Crime 101."

Quintin enjoyed that. He actually laughed.

French toast, bacon, coffee, juice, butter and syrup all went on the table. Skyler didn't sit but instead started making another batch of French toast.

Every once in a while, she froze briefly as it hit her again that they were actually sitting and eating at her table—horrible men, men who were probably killers—and she was serving them while they sat calmly beside her children.

It was unbearable.

But it had to be borne.

"So when are you putting the turkey on?" Quintin asked.

She hesitated, then turned to face him. "Soon, so I can make sure it's fully cooked before the genera-

tor starts to run out of gas. Actually, we should probably start trying to conserve a little now, so we can
be sure of having light and heat tonight."

"We could turn off more lights, turn down the
heat," Frazier said.

"No," Quintin said.

And there it was. Unspoken but clear.

Quintin didn't care if they lost power later. He
wouldn't be here.

And they wouldn't need it.

Uncle Paddy suddenly spoke up, breaking the chilly
silence that had settled over the room after Quintin's
comment. "It's Christmas. Let's open the gifts."

"Yeah, let's open the gifts," Scooter said. "No, wait.
Why should I care about presents? It's not like I'm
getting any."

"I told you, we always have extra gifts," Skyler said.

"What? A fruitcake?" Scooter demanded sulkily.

Skyler actually laughed, shaking her head. "No,
nice gifts."

"Don't you have to be good all year for Santa to
bring gifts?" Quintin asked. "I think Scooter has
been really naughty, don't you?"

Is he actually making a joke? Skyler wondered.

"Ignore him. I love getting presents," Scooter said.

"So where are these gifts?" Quintin asked.

"Normally, they'd already be under the tree," Skyler said.

"But this isn't 'normally,' is it?" Quintin said meaningfully.

"Most of them are in my room."

"And our rooms," Frazier said.

"We can all go upstairs, then," Skyler said.

"No. Scooter, you're in the kitchen with Mom," Quintin said. "Blondie, you stay here, too, and help with the clean-up."

"I can help in the kitchen, too," Kat said.

"Not you," Quintin told her.

"But—"

"Not you."

"Where am I this time, Quintin?" Craig asked.

"With me."

"You still don't trust me," Craig said.

"Smart guy for a college dropout," Quintin said. "Let's go."

As they left the kitchen, Brenda started bringing

plates over to the sink. "Thank you for breakfast, Mrs. O'Boyle," she said politely. "It was delicious."

Skyler almost broke out in laughter at the insanity of the situation, but she managed not to. "Thank you, Brenda. I'm glad you enjoyed it."

"Yup, that was great," Scooter said and he was smiling at her, almost like a kid.

A kid with a gun pointed right at her.

"Thanks," she answered, feeling she had to say something or risk his mood turning ugly.

"Are you going to get the turkey ready?" he asked excitedly.

"As soon as this is all picked up," she said.

With Brenda helping her, the work went quickly. While Brenda was getting out the special Christmas dishes with the trumpeting angels on them, Skyler realized she couldn't stuff anything more into the garbage bag.

She tied it shut, then started for the basement door without thinking. She caught herself quickly, hesitated, then said, "Scooter?"

"Yeah?"

"Is it all right if I dump the garbage in the basement?"

He frowned. "Quintin'll be mad if I—"

"All I have to do is open the door and toss it down, just so it's out of the way and won't stink up the kitchen."

He looked at Brenda, who was getting out more dishes, her back to him. "Yeah, sure go ahead."

Skyler nodded and walked across to the pantry, then past the servants' stairway. She could hear voices from upstairs.

"It's just a big box," Jamie was saying. "Honest, it's not dangerous."

"All right, all right," Quintin growled.

"If you want Scooter to open those extra gifts my wife was talking about, you're going to have to let me open that closet door," David said.

Shaking her head, feeling the sting of tears in her eyes, Skyler pulled open the basement door and almost screamed aloud, stunned to see two faces looking up at her. As it was, it felt as if her heart came to a dead halt in her chest.

Help had arrived.

Sheila Polanski and a young man she hadn't seen before. He had to be the deputy Sheila had brought with her the night before. They were standing at the bottom of the stairs; they had clearly been listening to what was going on upstairs.

Sheila brought her fingers to her lips, and Skyler knew. They were waiting. Waiting for the right time.

"Hey, what's taking you so long?" Scooter asked accusingly.

"I'm not taking so long," she protested, looking in his direction and tossing the garbage bag down the stairs. She didn't dare look, but she was sure the two deputies were quick enough to dodge it.

She was trembling so hard that she was afraid Scooter would notice. She didn't dare look at him. Instead, she headed straight for the refrigerator and opened the door.

She nearly jumped when she felt Scooter right behind her, and she turned, gulping.

"What the hell is the matter with you?" he demanded.

"You scared the hell out of me," she told him.

"Sorry," he said, and grinned, then glanced over at Brenda, who had turned, wide-eyed. "She's getting out the turkey," he said happily.

"Right. Where do these little plates go, Mrs. O'Boyle?"

"You can leave them on the counter until we set up for dinner," Skyler said.

"Where's the stuffing?" Scooter asked, looking deeper into the refrigerator.

"I make it separately."

"Why?"

"Because I don't put it in the turkey. Bread crumbs suck up moisture, and I want the turkey moist."

"Good thinking," he said approvingly, beaming at her.

She glanced past him toward the pantry. The door to the basement was ajar, and Sheila was visible just behind it. Scooter's back was to the door, thank God, but Quintin...

Quintin was upstairs, with her family. And a gun.

She dropped the turkey, and Scooter stooped to pick it up. She took advantage of the second when his attention was distracted to shake her head vigorously. She could hear the group coming back down the stairs and knew the time wasn't right. The right time would be when they were all together. When both men were preoccupied and could be taken at once.

Scooter handed her the turkey and looked around, as if he thought he should have seen something, but hadn't.

"What's going on?" he asked suspiciously.

Just then the door to the kitchen opened and the rest of the family trailed back in, Quintin last, his gun in his hand.

"Presents are under the tree," Jamie said.

"And I found you the best present ever," Kat said, going over to embrace her mother.

"The cops are here," Skyler whispered while they were hugging.

"No way. *I* got her the best present," Jamie said.

"Any present from my children is always the best present," Skyler said, and she turned to hug him, too.

Frazier laughed. "Hey, maybe *I* got her the best present."

Looking across the room then, Skyler saw Scooter's

expression. It was deeply sad, and she read in his eyes that he intended to kill them all. Or at least that Quintin did and Scooter wasn't going to stop him.

But not until they'd had turkey.

"I'm not sure how brilliant this is," Sheila whispered, shivering as she hovered close to Tim in the basement.

"Hey, we're in, aren't we?" Tim said.

"Yeah, we're in, but…we're still in the same situation. How the hell are we going to get in position to take out both men at once without one of them shooting one of the O'Boyles?"

"Patience," he said.

Very little light filtered into the basement, just a little daylight coming through the grimy window, so Tim's face was in a shadow. And it was difficult, from down here, to hear what was going on above. If Skyler O'Boyle hadn't been alone coming to the door, they would have been caught. Neither of them had realized she was there until it was almost too late. They'd only made it back down in the nick of time.

"Patience is great. But when and how?" she murmured.

"Over turkey?" he asked.

She exhaled. "Oh God, Tim, we can't fuck this up. It'll be a bloodbath if we do."

"Clean shots," he said. "Scooter and Quintin."

"Over the turkey," she said.

"The turkey isn't going to care," he murmured, and then he frowned, listening intently.

The turkey had just gone into the oven, and he could tell from the footsteps that everyone had gone into the living room.

"Oh, wow!" Jamie cried delightedly, staring raptly from his gift to his parents, then back to the package he had just unwrapped. "You found it," he said incredulously.

Skyler, sitting in one of the upholstered chairs, smiled. "Your father found it."

"Kat, open yours," Skyler said.

"Why does she get to go next?" Scooter asked.

Kat turned to him. "We go by age. Jamie is the youngest. Then me."

"Aren't you and your brother twins?" Quintin asked.

"We are, but I was born first," Frazier said.

"So...what? You're five seconds older?" Quintin scoffed.

"Ten minutes, to be exact," Frazier said. "Besides, Kat is impatient. I'm not."

"You are so," she teased him.

"You're right. I *am* impatient. So open your box so we can get to mine."

"When do I get to open mine?" Scooter demanded.

"After Frazier. You're older than he is," Skyler said. Scooter sighed.

"Actually, Kat and I should both go after Brenda," Frazier said.

"Hey," Scooter protested.

"It's how we do Christmas," Kat said calmly.

"All right," Scooter said with a sigh.

He had a gun and could have demanded the right to open his present next, Skyler knew. But he didn't. Scooter really wanted this Christmas. A real Christmas. A family Christmas. Even if he intended to massacre her whole family after dinner.

Skyler almost smiled. He and Quintin didn't know about the cops in the basement.

"I can actually wait," Brenda said.

"Open your package," Scooter ordered.

"It's from the whole family," Skyler pointed out.

"Mom, do you mind if she opens the one from me first?" Frazier asked.

"Of course not," Skyler said.

And then she knew. Before Brenda even opened the box and squealed, she knew. It was an engagement ring.

Frazier hadn't even told them!

Maybe he had meant to. Maybe he hadn't had the chance. She caught his eyes and read the apology in them, and she knew he *had* meant to tell them, perhaps even ask for their blessing.

"Oh, Frazier," Brenda breathed.

"Will you marry me, Brenda?" Frazier asked softly.

"Yes, oh, yes," she said, and kissed him.

"Get a room, would you?" Jamie moaned.

Blushing, Brenda sat back. "Behave, almost brother-in-law," she said.

Skyler could hear her older son swallow. Frazier didn't know that help was waiting just downstairs and that they might survive. It had been extremely important to him that Brenda know he had gotten her the ring.

Because the wedding might never come to pass.

"That's a beauty," Scooter said, stepping closer to examine the ring.

Skyler noticed Craig watching the older man uneasily. Almost as if he were afraid Scooter was going to wrench the ring away from Brenda there and then. "All right," she said quickly. "I need to baste the turkey soon, so we should keep going, but, Brenda, Frazier, congratulations."

"Let's move on now," Scooter ordered. "Kat, open your present."

"I'm sorry, but I'm not sure your father and I managed to top Frazier's present to Brenda," Skyler warned her daughter. She was trying not to watch Craig, because Craig was still watching Scooter.

And Scooter was watching the ring.

Skyler felt a sudden knot in the pit of her stomach. They were probably jewel thieves. Which meant that they would definitely be stealing Brenda's ring. And the only reason they weren't stealing it right now was because they intended to wait.

Until after the turkey.

"My boots!" Kat cried delightedly, opening the box. She had seen this particular pair of knee-high, fur-lined boots in a boutique window over the post-Thanksgiving weekend, when she'd been out shopping with her mother. They'd been hugely expensive, so she had just sighed and walked away. But she had coveted them, and Skyler had seen that and gone back for them later.

"Well, they're bigger than the ring," Jamie said.

"Fine. They're great. Frazier, open your gift now. Do it," Scooter commanded.

"Is it all right if he opens his from me?" Brenda shyly asked Skyler.

"Of course," Skyler said, wondering if Brenda had bought Frazier a ring, as well.

But it wasn't a ring. It was a medallion. A beautiful, simple St. Christopher's medal in gold.

Once again, Scooter jumped out of his seat to admire it. And once again, when Skyler looked at Craig, she saw the tension in his features.

"Brenda…it's beautiful," Frazier told her.

"You two have great taste," Scooter noted. "Now me!"

"I think Craig is younger than you are," Skyler said firmly.

Scooter frowned. "You have a gift for him, too?"

"We don't always know who might stop by around the holidays," David said. "Skyler likes to be prepared."

"It's okay," Craig said. "I don't need anything. Let Scooter open his present."

Skyler followed his eyes and registered the way Quintin was just sitting and watching everything, his gun at the ready.

"No, you have a present, and you *are* younger than I am, so open it," Scooter commanded.

"Scooter…" Craig protested.

"It's Christmas, and we have to do Christmas right," Scooter said.

Such hopeful words, Skyler thought, and today, knowing what was to come, also so ominous.

Craig opened the box Skyler quickly handed him.

"This is perfect," he murmured, pulling out a deep blue cashmere scarf. "Absolutely beautiful. Thank you."

He looked at Skyler, and she smiled at him. She longed to say that she knew he wasn't with the monsters holding her family hostage. And then she felt a tightening in her stomach again. There were cops in the basement, cops who undoubtedly thought he was one of the criminals. Cops who, if they managed to save her family, might well kill him.

She looked away to hide her thoughts. She couldn't afford to care. Her family had to come first. And it was still far from certain that her entire family would survive what was to come.

What did she know, anyway? He had come here with the other two. He was one of them. Just the one…

With a conscience.

But she noticed that her daughter was looking at him, as well. And for a moment Kat looked as if she were going to cry.

How well had she known him? Skyler wondered.

"My turn!" Scooter insisted.

"Yes, Scooter, it's your turn," David said patiently.

"Which box is mine?" he demanded.

"This one," Paddy said, pushing a box toward Scooter with his cane.

Scooter didn't tear into the paper. He picked up the box and held it, studied it, as if awed by the wrapping alone.

"Great bow," he said. "Pretty paper."

"I wrapped it," Kat said.

He glanced at her with a quick smile. "Wow."

"Open the damn thing, Scooter," Quintin said.

"I'm getting to it. I'm getting to it."

He still didn't rip into the box. He carefully, painstakingly, removed the bow, the ribbon and then the tape. He folded the ribbon and the paper, and set them carefully aside, as if they were a part of the gift. Then he opened the box.

He stared at the contents, then looked up at Skyler. "Cranium," he breathed, almost in awe.

"You seem to like games," she said.

"It's great. It's the coolest Christmas present I've ever gotten." He hesitated, frowning, as if trying hard to remember. "It might be the only Christmas present I've ever gotten."

"Look underneath," Skyler said.

He did, and his eyes widened in wonder. "Trivial Pursuit," he said happily. "Quintin, look, two games."

"Great."

"Mom, it's over to you now," Kat said.

"We need to wait," she said, as she stood and walked in the direction of the kitchen. "I have to baste the turkey." She spoke more loudly than necessary, hoping the cops could hear her and would get back downstairs, if they'd come upstairs to listen better. She had no intention of accidentally betraying the blessed deputies who intended to rescue them. "If I don't baste that turkey, it will dry out, and you don't want a dry turkey, do you, Quintin?"

"That will be my present. The turkey," Quintin said pleasantly.

"I'd like a soda," Jamie said.

"I need water," Kat added.

"Should we all go into the kitchen?" Skyler asked Quintin calmly.

Quintin shook his head. "Scooter, take Mom into the kitchen. And watch her closely. Mrs. O'Boyle, when you come back, bring the kids something to drink."

Skyler shrugged. "All right."

What was it about Quintin? Did he know? Why did he insist on keeping them all split up?

Scooter followed her into the kitchen. On her way over to the oven, she noticed that the dishes Brenda had stacked on the counter had been moved slightly, as if someone had leaned against the edge and bumped them.

She tried to act normal as she opened the oven and tended to the turkey, but her heart was thundering. She wanted—needed—to get back over to the basement door, but she didn't have another trash bag to get rid of. And if she walked that way for no good reason, Scooter would no doubt follow her to see what she was up to.

"Mmm-mmm!" Scooter said.

She jumped. He was right next to her.

"Can't wait," he said, sounding just like a kid.

She was suddenly certain that she didn't need to open the basement door. They weren't down there anymore. So where the hell were they?

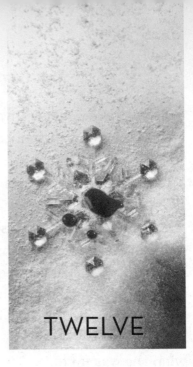

TWELVE

"Scooter!" Quintin shouted, then stared around the room impatiently. "How long does it take to baste a turkey?"

"I imagine Skyler's started the rest of the food," David said stiffly.

"We can all go in and see, if you want," Craig suggested.

"You can go to the door and find out what's going on," Quintin told him.

"Sure," Craig said. *What the hell kind of radar does Quintin have?* he wondered. The cops would need to get Quintin and Scooter together to take them out, which suddenly seemed impossible to manage. But he walked to the swinging door and did exactly as he had been told, just pushing the door inward and calling through, "Mrs. O'Boyle? What's going on?"

To his amazement, Scooter turned to him and announced proudly, "We're cooking."

Craig turned back to Quintin and said, "They're cooking."

"*They're* cooking? Scooter can't cook," Quintin said.

"Mrs. O'Boyle is teaching me," Scooter shouted happily.

Quintin stood. "I don't like this," he said, agitated. "Dad, you and the boys stay there. Uncle Paddy, in the kitchen. Blondie and Miss Troublemaker, you two get in the kitchen, too."

He'd seemed so calm, almost laid-back, when they were opening presents, but now, Craig thought, he was actively disturbed, even anxious.

Maybe worried that Scooter was beginning to like the family too much, that he wouldn't be able to do what was necessary when the time came.

"Where do you want *me,* Quintin?" Craig asked.

"Kitchen." Quintin narrowed his eyes. "I trust you about as much as I trust your redheaded girlfriend."

"I'm not his girlfriend," Kat said, her voice hard.

"You're a girl, and you were his friend," Quintin said impatiently. Craig swallowed, every muscle in his body seeming to clench, as Quintin reached for Kat, the gleaming silver nose of his gun aiming for her temple. "Everyone move," he barked.

Craig could see the agony that ripped at David O'Boyle as he watched his daughter being threatened and forced himself to remain in his chair. Meanwhile, Brenda and Paddy rose, ready to obey the order to move into the kitchen.

"Ye don't need to be manhandling me niece," Paddy said with dignity. "We'd know ye meant business without havin' to terrorize the lass."

"Just get in the kitchen," Quintin said.

"Scooter," Quintin snapped, holding the door open so he could see what was happening in both rooms.

"What?"

"Get the hell out here."

"But—"

"Get out here. And be on guard. Keep your safety off and your gun on Dad. Now."

Scowling, Scooter appeared. "Quintin, I was learning how to make candied yams."

"Eating them will have to be enough for you," Quintin said.

"Quintin, you don't have to make a misery out of dinner," Scooter said.

"Just get out here. I'm not going to make a misery out of anything. I just can't figure out how you can keep an eye on Mom if you're making candied yams."

Pouting, Scooter went out to the living room.

Craig walked past Quintin into the kitchen, Paddy and Brenda ahead of him. With an impatient sigh, Paddy took a seat at the table, setting his cane on top of it. Brenda paused by the sink, and Kat, shoved forward by Quintin, walked over to her mother's side.

"You're starting the rest of the food?" Kat asked.

Skyler nodded, looking as if she had just lost a negotiation she thought she should have won. "Yes. I was just putting the brown sugar on the yams. Brenda, would you start the green-bean casserole?

It's easy, just the beans, mushroom soup and then the fried onion rings. Everyone loves it. Unless they hate green beans. Or mushrooms. Or onions."

Skyler realized she was chattering on about nothing, just hoping to break the tension. But Brenda nodded and started on the casserole, while Kat took over the yams. Sighing, Skyler opened the oven to baste the turkey again.

Quintin took a seat next to Paddy, and Craig noted unhappily that someone sneaking up from the basement couldn't possibly get a clean shot at Quintin. Nor was he certain that anyone would have tried. He was sure Quintin was keeping everyone split up to make sure at least one O'Boyle would die, no matter what.

"So, Quintin," Craig said.

"What?"

"It's Christmas."

"Tell me something I don't know, college boy."

Craig forced himself to smile. "I was just thinking that we should have a drink to celebrate."

"It's early."

"Not in Ireland," Paddy offered.

"I'd even like a drink," Brenda admitted.

"Well?" Craig asked Quintin.

"What the hell. Go on."

As he stood to walk toward the counter where the liquor was kept, Craig felt Quintin's hostile gaze following him, and he sensed that Quintin was practicing his aim, the 9mm Smith & Wesson pointing right at his back.

That gun could blow a hole the size of a dinner plate right through him, and he suddenly and inconsequentially imagined himself as a cartoon character looking down at a huge hole in his stomach. He wondered vaguely if cartoons were still as violent as they had been when he was a kid.

"What'll it be?" he turned and asked the others.

"Whiskey, neat," Paddy said.

Quintin shrugged. "Same as the old Mick."

Craig poured the drinks, brushing by Kat. He couldn't believe that three years had passed. Three years and a staggering change in his life.

Craig set drinks in front of Paddy and Quintin. He wondered if it would be possible to somehow block Quintin's view of the others, forcing him to move and allow someone a good shot at him. But as he hovered, Quintin looked up at him suspiciously. Besides, he thought, if the two officers were in the house, which he had to believe was true, they weren't going to take a shot until the exact right moment. They wouldn't go for Quintin unless they had a clean shot at Scooter, as well. He moved back to the counter. "Brenda, did you want your whiskey neat, too?"

"Good God, no, you'll have to put something else in it for me," she said.

"Soda?" Craig asked.

"Sure. Cola, lemon-lime, whatever," Brenda said, intent on getting the last of the mushroom soup out of the can.

"You should never mix good whiskey with crap like that," Quintin said. "It'll give you a hell of a hangover. Not that it will matter."

A stunned silence followed his words.

Craig quickly handed Brenda her glass. She took it with shaking fingers, her blue eyes wide with fear.

He couldn't reassure her. Not at the moment. "Skyler, Kat…would you like something?"

Skyler shook her head, staring in at the turkey again.

Kat looked daggers at him. He knew she was wondering what the hell he was doing and letting him know she didn't want anything from him. Ever.

He poured himself a shot and went to sit next to Paddy. "Cheers," he said, and lifted his glass.

Paddy stared at him. *"Slainte,"* he returned.

Craig turned to Quintin. "They've seen us, you know," he said thoughtfully.

"What?"

Craig shook his head. "Those cops who came by last night. They've seen us. So when we leave here, after…whatever, they'll know we were here."

To his amazement, Quintin stared at him and blinked, and Craig realized that the other man hadn't realized the mistake he had made. He'd been obsessed with having this safe haven. He'd thought he had everything under control. And he hadn't realized what he had done.

Quintin sat perfectly still for a very long time, until finally Craig dared to speak out again. "It doesn't make sense to kill anyone here," he said.

Quintin smiled slowly, and he aimed the Smith & Wesson right at Craig's face. "But they didn't see *me,"* he said, and smiled malignantly. "And it won't make any difference to anyone if I kill you."

Would he have done it? Craig didn't know, because Skyler was suddenly right there, and she had clearly reached the end of her rope. "Stop it! I mean it. I have had it with the bickering and the backbiting, and I don't give a damn if it's you two or my own kids. Read my lips. *This is Christmas!* I'm cooking a turkey. And I am sick of the entire world behaving like a pack of two-year-olds. There will be no more fighting around this table, do you understand?"

Quintin was stunned. He just stared at Skyler, who stood over him, her hands on her hips, her eyes flashing.

He didn't shoot Craig, and he didn't shoot Skyler. And after a moment, he even began to laugh.

Craig could hear Kat's gasp of relief, and he looked over and saw her doubled over, shaking.

He stood. "Kat, are you sure you don't want a drink?"

"I can get it myself," she said, and turned away.

David O'Boyle sat on his chair, in his living room, with his Christmas tree and his sons, and stared at the man who was holding a gun on him.

Scooter seemed to feel he'd been duly chastised. He wasn't joking around, and he wasn't talking about Christmas. He only glanced toward the kitchen now and then, as if he were willing Quintin to come back.

They could all hear the rise and fall of conversation coming from the other room. *What's going on in there?* David wondered. To take his mind off the things he couldn't control, he turned to Scooter and asked, "How long have you worked for Quintin?"

"I don't work for Quintin," Scooter said, frowning.

"Oh?" David said politely. He folded his hands in his lap.

"I don't work for Quintin," Scooter repeated, more vehemently this time.

"Sure. I believe you."

"It's the truth."

"I said I believe you."

"You know, if anyone works for anyone…it was my thing first. My gig."

"Right," David said. "That's one hell of a gun you got there."

Scooter sneered. "What would you know about it?"

"I don't own a gun," David said, "but that doesn't

mean I don't know anything about them. I've heard the sales pitches, read about the laws. They always ask what you want a gun for. You know, are you a hunter? Marksman? Do you need it for self-defense? Strange, I never heard anyone claim they had the best gun for holdups and harassing innocent families. And killing, of course, but, hey, that's just an assumption."

A muscle started twitching in Scooter's jaw. "Shut up. Just…shut up. You know, if you'd had a gun, you could have shot me."

"And maybe Quintin would have shot half my family while I was doing that."

Scooter looked down, embarrassed, for a moment. "You got a nice family," he said when he looked up. "All you have to do is…well, don't try anything, okay?"

"Quintin plans on killing us, no matter what," David said.

"Now that's just not true," Scooter said, but he was a bad liar.

"He who lives by the gun dies by the gun," Jamie said.

Scooter only laughed. "No death penalty in this state," he said. "That's why I moved up here."

"From where?" Frazier asked.

"Louisiana. I went to Florida first, but then I figured a state without the death penalty would be best for me," he said. He sounded pleased with himself, as if he thought he'd been very smart to have figured that out.

"Scooter, has it occurred to you that a cop could shoot you?" David asked.

"Yeah. You're a nice guy, but a cop might not know that," Frazier said.

"I don't give cops a reason to shoot me," Scooter said. "I just hold up places when no one is there. I mean…" His voice trailed away.

"Do you actually know how to shoot, Scooter?" David asked.

"Of course! I shoot beer bottles all the time. Hey, don't you go thinking I'm easy. My aim is good. And this thing can blow a hole in you…well, you saw the lamp."

David felt ill. He thought he had understood

everything Scooter *hadn't* said. Scooter had never killed anyone. But Quintin had.

And Quintin was more than willing to do it again.

And no matter what Scooter said, he did what Quintin ordered, which meant that if he had to, Scooter would shoot any one of them to save his own hide.

"Beer bottles and people. Two different things," David said.

"But…" Scooter began, then fell silent.

"What?" David said. Scooter's mood swings were the scariest thing about the man.

Scooter was frowning and looking toward the stairs. "What the hell?"

"What?" David asked, alarmed.

Scooter stared at him. He was nervous, wound up and angry. "How the hell many kids do you have?"

"Three."

"No, really."

"I swear to you, Scooter. I only have three children."

"There was someone on the stairs."

"It must have been a trick of the light," David said, his heart thundering.

Craig had told him, when he'd tried to help him

after Quintin had bashed his face half in, that help would be coming. And Craig *had* been sitting next to Sheila last night…. He was afraid to breathe. Were the cops in the house? Was that why Skyler had looked at him strangely earlier?

"I saw something," Scooter insisted.

"A trick of light," David repeated.

"Quintin!" Scooter shouted.

Scooter was going to say something, David realized. And if he did, everything might be lost. He stood and said, "My God…"

"What?" Scooter demanded.

"Smell that turkey."

The kitchen door swung open and Craig appeared. Apparently Quintin was using him as his communications man. "Quintin wants to know what you're shouting about, Scooter."

"Turkey," David said. "It smells absolutely great. We were just wondering how soon dinner would be ready."

Scooter stared at Craig and frowned, as if he were trying to remember his train of thought.

"Scooter, what's up?" Craig asked.

"I don't want to be out here. I want to be in the kitchen," Scooter said.

"I'll tell Quintin," Craig told him.

The swinging door closed.

"I thought you didn't work for Quintin?" David said.

"I don't." He looked as if he were thinking about heading straight for the kitchen, but then he stopped. "I don't work for Quintin," he snapped. "But...we're a team. You know. Teammates!"

"Sure," David said.

"You're wrong. You're all wrong," Scooter told him.

"Whatever you say," David said.

"You have to understand. Quintin...he's my friend. He cares about me. So I have to be his friend. Show him I care about him."

"Friends don't hurt friends," David said.

"Or make them do things that will hurt them in the end," Frazier offered quietly.

"Quintin is my friend," Scooter insisted, his gun hand starting to shake.

"Whatever you say. We believe you," David said reassuringly.

"Smell that turkey," Jamie said encouragingly.

The nervous twitching in Scooter's fingers abated.

"Turkey, potatoes, gravy…and dessert. Lots of dessert, Scooter," Frazier promised.

Kat pretended it took great artistry to put the brown sugar on the yams, then sliced the butter into tiny increments to put on top, anxious to stay in the kitchen with her mother. Besides being constantly terrified, she was now completely confused.

Craig had purposely drawn out the truth they had all been trying to ignore—as if, by keeping quiet, they could keep it from being true. Then he had pointed out a fact that might actually save their lives.

And she…she was continually praying that the cops in the house would shoot Quintin and Scooter.

Was that a horrible thought? Wanting to see someone's brains blown out? Maybe, but after the way the two men had terrorized her family…horrible or not, it was there.

But what the hell was Craig really up to, and whose side was he on?

She had seen what he had done, trying to maneuver Quintin into moving and giving one of the cops a chance to shoot him, if they had split up and the other one had been able to get a bead on Scooter. But Quintin hadn't played along, and nothing had happened.

Had Craig somehow known nothing would happen? Was everything he was doing now just an act? Was he playing both sides against the middle, waiting to see who came out on top before jumping one way or the other? If Quintin and Scooter were able to escape, would he throw in with them and go, too? But if not, would he try to pretend he'd been a good guy the whole time, playing along with the gun-wielding duo just to survive?

Once upon a time she had adored him. She had gotten up every morning wanting to see him. She had done all the little things women did when they first fell passionately in love. Her legs were constantly clean-shaven. She had watched her diet, exercised, angsted over her imperfections, and she had marveled at the amazing fact that he was in love with her, too.

Lust had played a part, too. He had the kind of face that belonged on magazine covers. He was fit without being musclebound, and back in those days he'd sported a healthy tan. She'd watched him in class sometimes, hoping to meet him, then had been almost afraid to believe her luck when she did. They'd talked about spending spring break in the Bahamas, just the two of them. Renting a little cottage on a beach somewhere, diving, snorkeling, swimming, parasailing…making love in the waves, with a cool breeze wafting over them.

And then…

Cold, hard and fast, it had been over.

And, oh God, the heartbreak. To escape her pain, she'd done every stupid thing possible. Stayed out too late, drank too much, slept with the wrong guy just because he was on the football team. She seemed to remember that he'd been able to open beer bottles with his teeth. She wondered vaguely if he still had any.

She might even have gotten into drugs, but when she'd started on the wrong path, Frazier had suddenly thrust himself back into her life, yelling at her and, somehow, as her twin, suffering with her. Growing up, they had argued the way any siblings would, but when it mattered, he'd been there for her. He'd straightened her out.

And her mom… Back then, when she'd been in so

much pain after Craig's defection, her mother's every word, her concerned calls, had driven her crazy. But now—now more than ever, with life hanging by a thread—she had to wonder how she had ever been so cruel to someone who loved her so much.

And, of course, there was her father. Jamie. Even Uncle Paddy. They meant everything to her. Surely she couldn't lose them now.

It was suddenly very hard not to burst into tears as she thought about all the family stories and hoped she could remember them all to tell her own children one day, if she ever had any.

If she lived to have any.

Once she and Craig had talked about having kids, lying in each other's arms and musing about the future. He'd believed passionately that children needed a mother and a father, and said that he wanted at least two, because no one should have to be an only child. And he had believed that both parents should have dreams.

So what had happened to his dreams?

"What *are* you doing?"

She nearly jumped a mile, stunned to see that

Quintin had walked up without her noticing and was standing next to her.

"Yams. I'm making the yams."

"It looks as if you're trying to paint the Mona Lisa."

"Hey, this is Christmas dinner. It has to be perfect," she said, and looked around. She was alone in the kitchen with Quintin. Where had everyone else gone? And when?

"Get that in the oven," he said. "Let's go."

"Where are we going?" Her heart skipped a beat. She couldn't help it. Quintin scared the hell out of her.

He smiled, as if he knew and enjoyed the fact.

"It's Christmas, baby girl. And there are still gifts to open. Don't you want your mom and dad to get their presents?"

He touched her then, brushed her face with his fingers, and she thought she would scream, or fight or do something terrible that would get her killed, and then everyone else.

The swinging door opened, and Craig came in. A criminal? Or the boy next door?

Whichever, he had arrived at just the right moment. She tried to keep her heart from leaping. She couldn't forgive him now, not even if they were all going to die. Only an idiot forgave the person who had crushed her.

"Hey, Quintin, come on," Craig said impatiently. "Mrs. O'Boyle said we can eat in about an hour after Kat gets the yams in the oven."

Quintin took a step back and aimed the gun at her, then turned to aim it at Craig for a moment. "I call the shots," he reminded them both, then grinned. "The shots—get it?"

Kat turned her back on him and shoved the casserole dish into the oven, in the space left for it right beneath the turkey.

Upstairs, their backs against the wall of the hallway, Sheila hovered with Tim. They had quickly realized, once they were inside, that they weren't going to be able to rush up the basement stairs and shoot the men from the top step, so they'd crept up the back stairs when everyone was in the living room.

"Shit," Tim swore, glancing down the stairs.

"What?" she whispered.

"It's as if they know," Tim said.

"They don't know we're here," Sheila said. "I know that no one saw us come in."

"Maybe when Mrs. O'Boyle opened the door to the basement that Scooter guy sensed something," Tim said thoughtfully.

"It doesn't matter now. We've got to find a position where we can both get a clear shot," Sheila said.

"We'll never get a good chance at both of them."

"They'll have to get careless," she argued.

He nodded, then looked at her. "Sheila, we may have to…well, in the end, it might be better to take light casualties rather than—"

"No, don't say it," she warned him.

"We're running out of time," he said flatly. "We have to do something."

"Not yet."

"Sheila, can't you hear it?"

She swallowed hard. "You mean the storm."

"It's letting up."

"I know."

"In war, there are casualties."

"This is a house, not a war zone."

"Soldiers have to die sometimes."

"We're the only soldiers in here," she told him. "And we have a little more time. Plus we know the layout of the house now."

"So we're going with my plan then?"

She nodded, and he looked down toward the living room, then lifted his hand.

She slipped by him, hurrying for the landing of the servants' stairway.

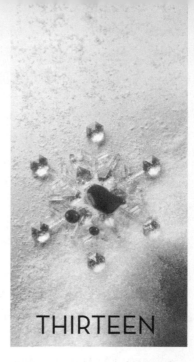

THIRTEEN

Craig tried desperately not to appear anxious, but he couldn't help wondering what the hell Sheila and Tim were doing and how much longer it was going to be before they made their move. Had they gone upstairs? Were they watching from the landing, as Kat had apparently done earlier?

The two of them had to be upstairs, he decided. And they had better move soon, because time was running out.

But how the hell would they ever get the opportunity when Quintin and Scooter seemed to be more on guard than ever, constantly surrounding themselves with members of the family to shield themselves at all times. But from *what?*

They couldn't know the cops were in the house, could they? He was absolutely certain Quintin hadn't seen the two deputies outside.

Every second was terrible.

Quintin had decided he wanted to hear more music, so Skyler was back at the piano. Scooter was on the bench next to her, protected by her. To reach him, a bullet would have to go through Skyler.

Clearly the tension was wearing on the family, as well. Skyler had played a few Christmas carols and everyone had joined in, but the performance had been lackluster, and now she was just sitting there, looking lost and defeated.

"What's the problem?" Quintin asked.

She shrugged. "I just…"

Suddenly a plaintively beautiful sound filled the air. Frazier, who was sitting on the floor by the tree, had picked up his violin. Skyler smiled, as if her son had given her a surge of energy. Her fingers moved over the keys, and she started to sing what sounded to Craig like an old folk melody. The entire family sang along, and then, to Craig's amazement, Scooter joined in on the last verse.

> The sailor gave to me a rose
> A rose that would ne'er decay
> He gave it so I'd be e'er reminded
> Of the time he stole my thyme away....

When the song ended, Scooter was staring at Skyler with tears in his eyes. "That's a sad, sad song," he said.

"You're depressing me," Quintin said, irritated. "Sing something else. Something cheerful. Let's have a happy Christmas carol," Quintin said.

"'Frosty the Snowman,'" Scooter insisted.

Then "Rudolph, the Red-Nosed Reindeer." Scooter liked that one, too.

Finally Quintin looked at his watch. "Enough," he said. "Mrs. O'Boyle, time for you to open something. But come over here, where I can see you."

Scooter, too, remained wary, and positioned himself directly behind Skyler. There was no way anyone could get a shot at him from the top of the stairs, Craig realized unhappily. He kept his attention on Scooter and was barely aware when Jamie handed his mother a box.

"Oh my God, I love it!" Skyler exclaimed, drawing his attention back to her. "It's wonderful."

The gift was a gold locket. The chain was thin, the locket itself small, of far less value than the jewelry Frazier and Brenda had exchanged. Value that Quintin and Scooter had assuredly already assessed. In fact, he was surprised Quintin was allowing them to live out their fantasy until after the meal. Did he intend to take that ring off Brenda's bloody fingers once he had shot her? He had to force himself not to look toward the stairway again, afraid of giving the game away.

"I put a picture of your parents inside," Jamie said.

"Oh, Jamie, what a wonderful gift," she told him, tears in her eyes, though she quickly blinked them away. She started to get up to hug her son.

"Sit," Scooter said. He seemed agitated, and he shrugged, as if confused as to why he had spoken out so quickly and vehemently.

Skyler looked at him questioningly.

"Just…just open the rest of your gifts," he said.

Quintin, frowning, looked over at him. "You all right, Scooter?"

"Yeah, sure."

Skyler continued opening her presents. Her gift from Kat was a delicate bracelet of diamond-chipped clovers. Frazier and Brenda gave her a cashmere shawl and a brooch, and Craig found himself getting more and more nervous about all the jewelry, but he didn't get really uneasy until she opened her gift from her husband. He had gotten her a diamond necklace, one with three beautiful and clearly valuable stones.

But as she exclaimed over it and thanked her husband, no one attempted to move.

"Dad, your turn," Frazier said.

As they began again, it seemed to Craig as if the O'Boyles were making a concerted effort to ignore their unwanted guests. The final gift was for Uncle Paddy, ten hot-stone massages.

"Now maybe you'll get through a day without complaining about the pain in your poor aching back," Kat teased him.

They were all laughing. Almost as if, for just a few

minutes, they had forgotten what was happening and were having a good time, just like any family at Christmas.

But that time was slipping away. Or rather, being stolen away, Craig thought.

But the cops were in the house, he reminded himself. There were two cops, himself, the family and Brenda.

How would they ever pull it off?

He thought that maybe Scooter was so strange because he was sad and just wanted a family. And the relationship between Quintin and Scooter was sort of familial, in a bizarre way. He glanced at Quintin, who was clearly growing impatient, then was surprised when Scooter suddenly stood up and pulled Skyler to her feet. "That turkey must be cooked by now. Come on, I want my Christmas dinner."

"Scooter, the turkey has to sit for a little while before I can carve it," David said.

"But we'll get it out of the oven *now,* right, Quintin?" Scooter demanded. "I'll take Skyler in, we'll get the turkey out. Now."

"Yes, fine," Quintin said. But he seemed distracted and stood very still for a minute. "Listen," he said softly.

"Listen to what?" Jamie asked.

"The wind," Quintin said.

"I don't hear it," Jamie told him.

Quintin smiled and said softly, "Exactly."

FOURTEEN

The turkey was a beautiful golden brown.

Everyone except Quintin and Scooter helped set the table, and then Kat put herself in charge of drinks, which gave her a chance to watch everyone as she went back and forth, filling glasses. Scooter was almost hyper with excitement, and Quintin, watching Scooter, grew visibly edgy.

When it was time to put the turkey on the table, Quintin took her mother's elbow and led her to a chair. "Someone else can carry the turkey. You'll sit next to me. Now."

Skyler shrugged. "Fine. David carves. See that the bird is in front of him."

"I want some skin," Scooter said.

"You can have all the skin you want," David said.

Everything was even tenser, even worse, than it had been, Kat thought, and all because the wind had stopped. The storm was winding down. Soon the plows would be out, and it would be time for Quintin and Scooter—and Craig?—to run. But before they ran…

"I've got the turkey," Kat said, and carried the bird over to the table.

"Let me," Craig told her, and managed to take the heavy platter and set it on the table in front of her father, who, she saw, was trying not to look at the carving knife too longingly.

"Wait," Quintin said. "Put that knife down."

"You have a better suggestion for how to carve a turkey? You want to do it yourself?" David asked Quintin.

Quintin stared at him steadily. "All right, carve. But I'll be watching you."

"First, grace," Skyler announced.

"Hurry up," Quintin told her, his patience visibly fraying.

"Thank you," she said, then bowed her head and spoke. "God is great, God is good, and we thank him for this food. Through Jesus Christ our Lord, Amen."

No sooner had she finished than Scooter shot up, waving his gun around. "Did you hear it?" he asked.

"Hear what?" Quintin demanded.

"That!"

"What?" Quintin repeated.

"There's someone in this house," Scooter claimed.

Quintin stood, grabbed Skyler by the hair, and dragged her out of her chair and out the door.

David leaped up to follow.

"Stop!" Scooter shouted, and when her father turned around in response and she saw his face pale, Kat suddenly realized that Scooter had his gun aimed right at her.

"Stop it, Scooter," Craig snapped, and to Kat's amazement, he stepped between her and the gun. "Come on, we have to see what's going on."

Before Scooter had time to object, Craig caught

him by the arm and pulled him out. In a rush, the family followed them into the living room, where Quintin was holding Skyler in front of him, a human shield, while he looked wildly around, brandishing his gun as if in search of a target.

Kat saw her father start to rush the other man, but Craig caught hold of him. Not hurting him, just stopping him.

"Everybody calm down," Craig pleaded. "Quintin, stop hurting her."

"I'll hurt her, all right. I'll put a bullet right through her head if whoever is up those stairs doesn't come down right this minute."

"Quintin, what the hell's the matter with you?" Craig demanded.

"Scooter isn't the sharpest tool in the shed, but he's like a damned dog," Quintin said. "If he says someone is up there, someone is up there." He raised his voice. "And whoever the hell it is needs to come down here. Now."

He cocked his gun, and the sound seemed louder than any storm.

"Now!" Quintin raged.

Kat held her breath, a rush of terror weakening her knees, threatening to make her pass out.

Her mother…

Quintin…

The gun…

"Get down here now or she's dead, and you will have killed her."

A split second passed. Then, from the second-floor landing, a male voice said, "Stop! Wait!"

Kat gasped in dismay, sucking in air, all hope lost, as Tim Graystone walked down the stairs, both hands high in the air.

"Throw your gun down," Quintin demanded.

"Let her go first," Tim said. Kat could see that he was trembling, but his expression was determined. And he was alone.

"I should just shoot her and be done with it," Quintin said disgustedly.

"Shoot me instead," Tim pleaded.

"Stop it! Don't shoot anybody," Craig thundered.

Amazingly, everyone in the room turned to stare at him. "Calm down, everyone. Quintin, please, let go of Mrs. O'Boyle. Officer, toss down your weapon. Come on, people."

"Put that gun down slowly," Quintin commanded.

"All right," Tim agreed.

Quintin eased his hold on Skyler as Tim set down his weapon on the floor right in front of Quintin.

"Get it, Scooter," Quintin said.

He didn't suggest that Craig take it, Kat noticed.

"Where's your partner?" Quintin demanded.

"My partner?" Tim said.

"I'm not stupid. Your partner, the woman who came with you last night. She's got to be around here somewhere."

"Oh, Sheila," Tim said.

"Yes, her. She needs to get down here right now."

"She can't. She's checking out a possible emergency," Tim said.

"You're lying."

"I'm not," Tim insisted. "It's just the two of us, and we had to split up."

There was a horrible, staggering moment then, when Quintin struck Tim with his gun. Hard. So hard that the young deputy fell back, crashing into the wall. Then he aimed at Tim. "Where's your partner?"

"Answering a call out by the highway."

Quintin took a step toward him. Aimed at his kneecap. "Where's your partner?" he repeated.

"You can shoot me to death piece by piece," Tim swore. "But I can't change the facts. She's on another call. I had a hunch something was wrong, but she thought I was nuts. Said she wouldn't come back with me because of the kid, not when there might be a real emergency."

"What?" Quintin demanded.

"He's talking about me," Jamie groaned. "I pulled a prank last year, pretended I needed help…. It's my fault."

Craig moved forward, standing between Quintin and the downed man. "Quintin, think about it. Don't you think she'd have come down here by now if she was in the house?"

Quintin stared back at Craig, lifted his gun and aimed at Craig's face.

"Go on, shoot me, then," Craig said impatiently. "That's not going to change the fact that she isn't here. And listen. It's the wind again. The storm hasn't stopped yet."

"It will. Soon," Quintin told him, narrow-eyed.

"We all need to calm down," Craig said quietly, facing Quintin, ignoring the gun only inches from his nose.

Quintin looked around the room. He was rigid and furious. Kat was amazed he hadn't fired yet. "I want him tied up. Tight." He kicked Tim for emphasis.

"We don't have any rope," Scooter said.

"Get that phone cord," Quintin said.

Craig went for the cord, ripping it from the wall.

"Tie him up, and don't fuck with me. Tie him tight," Quintin ordered.

"I won't fuck with you," Craig promised. Kat could see him looking at Tim with sorrow and a prayer for forgiveness.

Tim seemed to give him a little nod, as if to say, *You gotta do what you gotta do.*

"I want to see how you're tying him," Quintin said. "Scooter, you keep an eye on them."

"I will, Quintin. I've got my gun on them. I'll shoot the suckers, turkey or no turkey, I swear I will."

Quintin watched as Craig bound Tim with his wrists tightly behind his back. When he was done, Quintin started to laugh.

"What the hell…?" Craig said.

"Cuffs. He's a cop. We should've just used cuffs. Oh, well, you did a good job. Now bring him into the kitchen, so we can keep an eye on him while we eat."

No one moved; tension held them as if they were glued in place.

"Move!" Quintin snapped. "Help Craig bring the cop in the kitchen," he added, turning to Frazier.

Frazier stared back at Quintin for a moment, then hurried to Tim Graystone's other side, helping to support him.

In the kitchen, they all took their places again, after Craig and Frazier had used an old extension cord to tie Tim Graystone to the banister of the servants' staircase.

"Serve the turkey," Quintin said to David.

David looked at Quintin. "White or dark meat?" he asked, hatred and fury thick in his voice.

"White."

Somehow everyone was served, but nobody made a move, despite the food on their plates.

"Eat," Quintin said.

Skyler took a forkful of turkey, stared at it, then set down her fork. "I can't eat. And I won't."

"You know, I have been a patient man," Quintin said. "But you're going too far."

Skyler leaned forward and met his eyes. "Am I? You're the one who plans to kill us. All of us. You've only waited because…well, I don't know why. Maybe you didn't want the mess while you were hiding here. Maybe so Scooter could have Christmas. Who knows? But all this time you've made us dance like puppets so we can live a little bit longer. You can make us sing, make us open presents, but you can't make anyone enjoy a Christmas dinner. You can't make me swallow when there's a lump in my throat the size of Texas. Not when a good man is hurt and tied to the banister."

"A good man?" Quintin mocked.

"A good man," she repeated.

"And what makes a good man?" Quintin demanded, sneering. "Being a cop? Bull. A good man is one who knows who to trust—and who not to trust. Who can be trusted by those who depend on him."

"And by that definition, Tim Graystone is a good man," Skyler said.

"I care about Scooter. Does that make me good?" he taunted.

"If you want me to think you're a good man, let Tim come sit at the table and have something to eat," Skyler said.

"Don't be ridiculous," Quintin snapped.

"Quintin, you can keep him tied up," David suggested. "But let him come to the table and one of us will feed him."

"Or none of us will be able to eat," Skyler said.

"I don't understand you at all," Brenda said suddenly, startling them all. She smiled and looked at the ring on her finger, then over at Frazier. "Here," she said, taking off the ring and setting it in front of Quintin. "You're thieves, right? I mean, you were going to take it before you left, anyway, right? I don't even want to think about how."

"Brenda…" Frazier said, his voice breaking.

"Frazier, it's all right. Let him take the ring.

Quintin, it's just a thing, a symbol, but whether I have it or not, I know Frazier worked hard to buy it." She smiled. "And I know he did it all on his own, because I could see by his parents' faces that they didn't know anything about it. You can take it away, you can even take away our lives, but what Frazier and I feel…what we have…no one can ever take that away. And no matter what happens, I feel sorry for you."

Quintin just stared at her, reduced to speechlessness for a moment, but then he reverted to form and said, "Very nice. Now, everybody, shut up and eat."

Scooter, oblivious to the mood around the table, dug in, delighted with his breast meat covered with the perfectly roasted skin, but nobody else did anything except push the food around on their plates.

"Shit. Get the damn cop, then," Quintin snapped.

Craig got up to go for Tim Graystone, and Quintin sent Scooter to find a chair. It didn't look to Kat as if Craig and Tim exchanged any words as Craig helped him to the table. Skyler stood as they neared the table.

Once Tim was settled, Quintin looked at Kat. "You're still not eating."

"I'm not hungry."

To her surprise, he leaned forward accusingly. "You ungrateful bitch," he told her. He leaned back again, staring around the table. "You all think I'm a monster, don't you? And maybe I am. But it's people like you made me one."

"No," David said. "We all have to take responsibility for what we become."

"Easy for you to say. You have everything."

"I didn't have everything," David said. "My parents were immigrants and worked nonstop all their lives. I started mowing lawns when I was thirteen and dragging ice for a soda fountain when I was sixteen. I've worked my whole life, too."

"No, no, you don't get it," Scooter said.

"Shut up, Scooter," Quintin said.

But Scooter ignored him and went on. "It's not always about money."

"That's a strange comment, comin' from a gun-carryin' thief," Paddy put in.

Scooter barely afforded him a glance. "You really don't understand. Quintin's mother, she was a prostitute. She didn't know who his father was. And she couldn't really keep him herself, so he went to a foster home."

"Scooter…" Quintin said warningly.

"Some folks just take in kids because when you take in kids, you get money. It's a lousy thing for a kid to end up there. Really lousy."

"Scooter, I'm going to shoot you in about ten seconds," Quintin threatened.

"Now my mother," Scooter continued. "Hell, she just drank. Drank and beat the tar out of me. By the time I was about fourteen, I'd had a dozen broken bones and I'd had to sit in the bathroom about eighteen million times while she slept with her latest guy. The first time I stole, it was for her. She wanted a bottle of vodka. I never looked back." Scooter waved his fork. "So then I'm seventeen, and I get hauled into court, and they decide they're not going to try me as a juvenile. So I wind up in prison, with a pack of big-ass jerks, and when I get out, guess what? No one wants to hire you when you've been in jail. So I go home to my mother. Then, I don't know what happened. She was drinking and yelling at me and waving the vodka bottle around. I swear to God, she fell. I didn't kill her. The bitch deserved it, but I didn't kill her. Hey, can I have some more gravy, please?"

They were all dead still, just staring at him. Then Kat heard her mother gulp. "Jamie…the gravy. Please."

"I know your life was awful," David said to Scooter. "But you can change it."

Quintin started to laugh. "Fuck you, O'Boyle."

David turned to Quintin. "And you. You think you can blame everything you do the rest of your life on being brought up in a lousy foster home."

Quintin laughed bitterly. "Let me think. Yeah, I do."

"We all make choices in our lives," David said stubbornly.

"Right," Quintin said. "How about you, college boy? What's your story? Make it a good one. Maybe I'll fall for it."

Kat couldn't help it. She stared at Craig, too. *What is your story?* she wondered. *Make it a good one and maybe I'll fall for it, too.*

Craig shrugged. "Mine is easy. Cocaine," he said.

"You aren't a cocaine addict," Kat said, staring at him.

He smiled slowly, ruefully. "No. I didn't mean me." He hesitated. "My dad. He didn't start off that way. Then…I'm not sure what came first, Alice Diaz or the drugs. Anyway, long story short. One day this man came to see me. He told me my dad owed him a lot of money, and he was going to kill him if he didn't get the money. What was I supposed to do? It was my *dad*," Craig said. "It was the drugs that changed things. And I knew he could change back."

"I think you ought to get your violin," Quintin said dryly to Frazier.

"Shh," Scooter said. "This is a good story."

"Go on," Kat told him.

He shrugged. "Well, I was a student with a part-time job. There wasn't any way I could get the kind of money they wanted. They knew that, of course. They had a plan for me. They'd wanted my dad to do it, but he wasn't in shape, so I was the next best thing."

"What was the plan?" Scooter demanded eagerly.

"My father had worked for a security company till he got so drugged-out he lost his job. He'd installed the system for a jewelry store. They got the information from him, then took me with them. I think I was like insurance for them, to make sure my dad wouldn't lie to them. They told him they'd kill me if he didn't tell them how to get past the alarm, and they told me they'd kill *him* if I wouldn't help them. So I did." He hesitated. "Then they shot me. But they didn't do it right, so I lived. But they cleaned the place out and killed the owner. And then they killed my father anyway."

There was silence.

Craig was staring at Kat.

She stared back. *Why didn't you tell me?* she asked silently. *Why didn't you go to the police?* But she knew. She knew when your family was threatened, you were ready to do just about anything. You would kill for them.

And you would die for them.

"Hear, hear!" Paddy said, breaking the silence.

They all stared at him. Either he was drunk, or he was doing a great job of pretending to be, Kat thought.

"Uncle Paddy, you've had enough," Skyler said gently.

"Good God, not nearly enough, me lass," Paddy

protested. "A man should be totally drunk before being shot."

"No one is going to shoot anyone," Craig said. Quintin stared at him, arching a brow.

"It doesn't make any sense to shoot anyone," Craig went on, and indicated Tim. "Don't you understand? His partner didn't come with him, but she knew where he was going."

"It's true," Tim agreed.

"It's like I said before, killing these people won't change anything," Craig finished.

"I think we should have dessert now," Quintin said, as if Craig hadn't spoken.

"What?" Craig asked, confused.

"I believe Tim's partner is in this house. I figured we'd go ahead and have dinner, and then I intend to find her. Of course, finding her won't be all that hard. I'm sure she's within earshot right now. But she knows she can't possibly get both of us, so she's not going to try anything. So…dessert."

They all just stared at him.

"Dessert," Quintin repeated. "Now."

Kat felt her heart was sinking.

The police had failed, and the end was coming.

And now…

Craig looked at her, held her gaze and mouthed something she couldn't make out.

She frowned. What was going on? What was he doing?

"May I serve?" Skyler asked.

Quintin grunted.

She looked at him. "Pumpkin or pecan?"

"Pecan for me, with ice cream," Scooter said.

"Craig?" her mother said after serving Scooter.

"Pumpkin," he said.

"Ice cream?"

"No, thank you."

Skyler set a piece of pumpkin pie down in front of Craig. "Looks great, Mrs. O'Boyle," he said casually and picked up his fork, then shouted. "Duck!" as he stabbed his fork into Scooter's hand, pinning it to the table.

The entire family went down, gasping…shouting…screaming.

Above the cacophony, Kat heard the explosion of a gun, and she dared a peek over the table.

Quintin was staring at her...staring... But he didn't raise his gun. Instead, it slipped from his fingers. His head crashed against the table, a hole in the back of it. Blood started to pool over his dessert plate and onto the tabletop.

Scooter was still screaming, a high-pitched and hysterical sound. Though one hand was still pinned to the table by Craig's fork, he had his gun in his other hand and was trying to aim, trying to shoot.

Craig had leaped across the table to throw himself on the man and the gun, but he didn't have to.

Kat heard a horrible snapping sound, and Scooter started screeching at an even higher pitch, his arm dangling at an unnatural angle. Uncle Paddy was standing next to him, his cane in his hand. He had used it to break Scooter's arm. Craig quickly reached over and picked up Scooter's gun. He immediately flipped on the safety and slid the gun into his waistband.

"Oh God," Skyler breathed. "Oh God," she said again, and started to cry.

Despite the confusion, Kat realized that Quintin had been right about one thing: Sheila Polanski had been in the house all along. Now she came running out of the pantry and into the kitchen.

"Is everyone all right?" she asked anxiously.

The question seemed so ridiculous under the circumstances that Kat almost started to laugh. A dead man was bleeding all over the table, and Scooter was still pinned and screaming.

To her horror, Kat did start to laugh.

Then she was hugging Sheila Polanski and her brothers, and someone was untying Tim Graystone, and she was holding Brenda and they were both sobbing. The next thing she knew, she was in her mother's arms, and then her father's.

It seemed as if the hysteria, the mix of laughter and tears and hugging and kissing, went on forever, and the whole time, Sheila's question kept running through her head.

Was everyone all right?

Kat didn't think they would ever be all right again.

Then she saw Craig. Saw him watching her. And she knew that while they might never exactly be all right, they would be better.

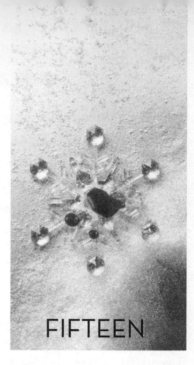

FIFTEEN

For a while time moved in slow motion, full of sounds and visuals Skyler knew would haunt her forever.

There was the sound of Scooter's screams. There was a look on his face, in his eyes. She had no doubt that he would have killed them if Quintin told him to. He had genuinely longed for and enjoyed his Christmas, but he would have obeyed Quintin without a second thought.

Another image... The remnants of a turkey dinner, gravy boat still on the table...pies out, ice cream melting...

Quintin's head, bleeding onto his plate.

So much confusion, the storm slowing but not gone, and the need—the bone-deep need—to get out of the house before she went mad. Scooter had been tied up, and Brenda saw to his wounds while he continued to howl.

They had to get out, Skyler thought. She knew she couldn't stay in the house that night.

She knew that, as long as she lived, she would never forget the way Quintin had died, never forget the blood flooding out over the table.

And all of her life she would be grateful that the blood had been Quintin's, that, miraculously, her family had all survived.

The wind finally began dying down for good. Sheila or Tim must have managed to get a signal and make a call, because, to her amazement, it wasn't long before they heard movement outside and realized that the state police had arrived and the house was surrounded.

It seemed impossible. As detectives and crime-scene investigators filled her house, all Skyler could think was that it must have been a dream. A nightmare. They had lived those hours so intensely, and then…

So quickly, it all seemed so impossible.

She couldn't mourn Quinton, but she almost felt badly for Scooter. Almost. The threat against her family had been far too terrifying for her to feel anything that resembled forgiveness for him yet, but maybe the time would come.

Skyler *had* feared for Craig when the police got there. She had been ready to testify that, whatever he had done in the past, he wasn't a killer and had in fact been ready to die for her family.

But the police didn't take him away. Instead they started to talk to him as if they knew him, knew all about him.

Tim was the one who explained it all to her. "I knew I had seen his face," he said, grinning. "And I finally remembered. He works with the state. He graduated from the state police academy with one of my buddies. I'd seen him in their graduation photo."

"So...he *was* a cop. All along," Skyler said.

"All along," Tim agreed, amused by her choice of words.

They *were* rather foolish, she thought. He hadn't suddenly become a cop in the midst of everything.

Tim looked at her and took her hands. "I'm sorry we couldn't get to you sooner. I don't know how that guy Scooter knew I was up there."

Skyler shrugged. "He… I don't know. He had an instinct."

"Yeah, well, that almost blew the whole thing. I still don't know why the other guy, Quintin, didn't just shoot me."

"He wanted his turkey dinner," Skyler said.

"Can someone really want a turkey dinner *that* badly?" Tim asked.

"It wasn't the dinner, exactly. Quintin wanted what Scooter wanted, and Scooter wanted…Christmas."

"What an elusive wish," Tim said.

The whole family had to be questioned. Nicely, but still, it seemed to take forever. The punishment for survival was always paperwork, one of the officers joked.

There were even moments of levity, despite the horror of having to relive everything.

At one point Jamie suddenly stopped in the middle of answering a question and asked to be excused to brush his teeth. It was the little things, she thought. They could be so important.

Eventually she saw the body taken from the house on a gurney, zipped into a body bag. Even then, she couldn't bear the thought of going back into the kitchen. She wasn't sure she could ever return to the kitchen.

There were people everywhere. It was early evening when they finally finished asking questions and filling in reports. When they were gone at last, she looked outside and stared at the blanket of fresh white snow, gleaming in the moonlight. From somewhere she could hear a Christmas carol playing.

God rest ye merry gentlemen,
Let nothing you dismay,
Remember Christ our savior was born on Christmas Day
O, tidings of comfort and joy
Comfort and Joy
O, tidings of comfort and joy.

Warm, strong hands fell on her shoulders, and she turned. David was standing behind her, and he took her in his arms. He started to speak, then stopped.

"It's all right," she said.

"No, it's not," he told her, and smiled awkwardly. "We all…I guess we all start out like Frazier and Brenda. With our hopes and our dreams—swearing to one another that we'll never be like our parents. And then…" He paused, smiling ruefully, shaking his head. "We let things stop us. Small problems become big ones. We see things in different ways, and we assume we can't change, so things fester and grow and…and I was angry that Frazier wouldn't hold the Christmas tree straight. It honestly never occurred to me that he was holding it the best he could."

She looked up at him, searching his eyes. "David…who cares about the Christmas tree right now?"

His smile deepened. "I don't. It isn't anything to do with the Christmas tree. It's life."

She realized she was shaking. "We're alive, David. Our kids are alive," she said.

"And I'm wondering if I deserved to survive," he told her.

She gasped.

"Don't misunderstand…I'm grateful But I keep remembering how strong everyone was, how our kids must have been terrified, but they didn't fall apart. Skyler, *we* survived this. We survived it as a *family.* That's…that's what I didn't deserve."

She touched his face. "But we *are* a family. Not one of us is perfect. No one can be. We have to…we have to just do our best and…stumble along. That's the journey."

"What if we hurt others on our journey?" David said. "When I think about the things I've said, the things I've gotten mad about…"

"David, all we can do is the best that we can, love the best that we can. I'm not suddenly going to become a perfect mother because of today, and you're not going to become the perfect father. But we will be smart enough to know that our lives are a gift, that our children are a gift."

"I do love you."

"I know," she assured him. "Christmas," she murmured. "I always thought it was such a time of promise…."

"And it is," he told her huskily.

"Hey, Dad!" Jamie shouted from upstairs. "Guess what? Tim's mother has a huge house, and Tim just talked to her. He didn't think we'd want to stay here tonight, so she's invited us all over."

David looked up. "That's nice of her, but there are too many of us to—"

"Mrs. Graystone says the more there are the merrier," Sheila said.

"Mom, Dad, please?" Jamie asked.

Skyler looked at David. "I sure as hell don't intend to stay here tonight."

They were all trying hard, Kat knew. Tim's mother, Lydia Graystone, was trying harder than anyone, taking in their entire entourage for a *real* Christmas dinner, on top of her own family and the people she'd already invited over, including Sheila.

Lydia insisted she was happy for the company, and as Kat helped her set up for her turkey dinner—one that she could eat, she was certain, because she was starving now—she thanked her for her generosity.

"It's the least I could do. When Tim told me what happened…" She broke off, shivering. "You have quite an amazing family."

Kat moved to the doorway and leaned against it,

looking out into the other room. She had to smile, and not only because her parents looked like newly-weds or because Frazier and Brenda were clearly oblivious to anything but each other. Not even because Tim had a sixteen-year-old sister, Olivia, and she and Jamie seemed to have hit it off as if they were long-lost friends.

But because of Uncle Paddy. Their hero.

He didn't seem to consider himself a hero, but she was certain Craig would have died trying to save them if it hadn't been for Paddy and his cane. But to Paddy, it had simply been something that needed to be done and he'd been there to do it. According to him, life was something you fought for, every immigrant new that. She smiled, aware of a new appreciation for her uncle and her ancestry that would remain in her heart for-ever. And Uncle Paddy was smiling at the moment, too, deep in appreciation of Sheila's company.

They had just sat down at the table when the doorbell rang.

There was a collective gasp from her family, and she wasn't surprised when her mother croaked, "Oh God. Don't answer it!"

Tim Graystone set his hand on her mother's shoulder. "It's okay," he said, and went to see who it was. A minute later, he came back. "Kat?"

"Yes?" She stood, and her heart took flight as she allowed herself to hope.

"An old friend wants to see you," Tim told her, and she knew without being told who it was.

Craig.

She wanted to see him.

She didn't want to see him.

You couldn't go back. She knew that, and knew, too, that she had no real idea what had gone on with him in the last few years, but…

She set her napkin down. "Excuse me," she told the group around the table and fled.

He was waiting for her on the spring porch. Somewhere along the way he had taken a shower and changed clothing, and he was in jeans, boots, a flannel shirt and a heavy wool coat. His hair was sparkling clean, light as straw, soft against his forehead. His eyes were very blue, very deep, serious.

She kept her distance. "I was wondering if we would see you again," she said politely. Oh God, how ridiculous that sounded. She swallowed and tried again. "I'm sorry. I really thought at first that you were with…them. It fit with the way you left school…and there was a rumor at one point that you were in jail."

"Yeah. I started that rumor. It made things easier," he said.

"I'm glad to see you."

"Are you?" he asked, and she wondered if there was a hopeful tone in his voice.

"To thank you for all you did. We're probably all alive because of you."

He lowered his head for a moment, then met her eyes again. "I think we're all alive because of *all* of us," he said.

She shrugged. "Maybe. You might have had a better chance of surviving if it weren't for us, though," she told him.

"Who knows?" he said. "I think Quintin had me pegged from the start. It was the first 'job' I did with them. And I'm pretty sure he knew I wasn't what I pretended to be."

"Still, thank you."

"You're welcome."

He was still looking at her. She shook her head. "You had no right not to tell me the truth."

"That my father was a cocaine freak and loan sharks were going to kill him if I didn't help them rob someone?" he asked softly.

"I loved you. You're not your father. You're not your family."

He looked doubtful. "I think in a way we *are* our families," he said. "You're a lot like both your parents," he said with a smile. "And yes, I remember you used to tell me how they could drive you nuts, but even so, I mean it as a compliment."

"Tonight, I'll take it that way." She paused, then met and held his eyes. "I would have understood you were having problems, you know."

"Your parents owned a bar. My father had gotten into knocking them over."

"I still wish you had believed in me, told me. It would have hurt less."

She was right. He had owed her. But he had been young then, with a young man's sense of pride and shame. And it *had* been a pretty desperate situation, and Kat, being Kat, would have gotten involved.

Her life, too, would have been at risk if he hadn't walked away.

But that was all in the past. Who knew what might have happened if they'd taken different forks in the road, made different choices?

"I'm sure you're welcome to have dinner here, too," she told him.

He shook his head uneasily. "I just…needed to see you."

She nodded, looked at him…remembered. And remembering hurt. "We can't go back," she whispered vehemently to herself—but he heard, too.

"No. We can never go back. And, oddly enough…I'm not sure I *would* go back, even if I could. I'd certainly never relive today, but…I'm so sorry I hurt you."

"You did hurt me. You devastated me. But I accept your apology. It's just that…like I said, we can't go back."

He nodded, but he was still staring at her steadily. "We can go forward, though," he said very softly.

She studied him. In the background, she could hear a Christmas carol playing, accompanied by her brother's violin. She had to smile. Unbelievably, she actually felt like laughing. Life was good, so damn good. And she would remember that.

"Come to dinner," she told him.

He hesitated. Inhaled, exhaled.

She offered him her hand. "All you have to do is take a step forward."

He grinned. Accepted her hand. And they walked in to Christmas dinner together.

EPILOGUE

"It's Christmas Eve," the man said.

The younger Hudson of Hudson & Son looked so much like his father that, for a moment, Craig thought he'd lost his mind.

He hadn't expected the shop to be open. Sheila had told him that before his death, Lionel Hudson had been intending to close the shop and move west to be with his son.

This Hudson wasn't a spring chicken, either. He looked like his father, but at the age of sixtysomething rather than eighty-plus.

"I know. I'm sorry. You're trying to close up. I just saw the sign and…"

Hudson frowned, looking at him. "You're Craig Devon, aren't you?"

Craig was startled. "I—yes." He felt awkward. Guilty. "I'm so sorry about your father."

Hudson nodded, studying him, then offered his hand. "I'm Ethan Hudson. I heard you tried to save my father."

The man was looking at him with such appreciation that Craig felt like a fraud, but he had to say something.

"I didn't know that…I didn't know they would kill anyone. I am so sorry. I should have been more prepared. I—"

"Please," Hudson said, and smiled. "I've heard all about it from Sheila and Tim. You're a good man. I know you would have saved him if you could. I've thought about it a lot, though. He wouldn't have wanted to waste away, to die in agony. Who knows what's for the best?" He shrugged, then grinned. "I remember him with love. That's the important thing."

"I thought the store was closing," Craig said.

"Funny, I thought so, too. But then Dad…died and I came back, and I'm still here. I'm glad, too. I loved this place when I was a kid. I'd sit on my dad's lap when he'd take out his magnifying glass and study a stone. In a way, working here, running this place, I feel like he's still with me." He offered Craig a strange and rueful smile. "Sometimes you learn what really matters, huh? I remember one time, there was a ring a woman wanted to sell. Even I knew the stone wasn't a good stone, but my dad paid her really well for it. And afterward he told me that what's valuable in life isn't things, it's what those things mean to people and what can be made of them." He paused, then said, "Sorry, I guess Christmas Eve is making me nostalgic."

Craig looked away for a moment, then said, a question in the words, "The sign…it still reads Hudson & Son."

"One of my boys moved out here with me, and he works here, too. He's off tonight, though. He has little kids and, well, you know. It's Christmas

Eve, he's got a lot to do. I needed to be here alone today, anyway."

"Yeah," Craig said huskily, feeling awkward again. He cleared his throat and looked into the jeweler's cases. "You've got some beautiful pieces here."

"Thank you."

"That solitaire…"

"Are you thinking about getting married?"

Craig looked at him and felt the oddest little tug in his heart. Was he thinking about it? Hell, yeah!

But was *she*?

He was scared. He knew all too well how many things could be stolen. Possessions, of course. Even life. But not the things that mattered in life, not unless you let them be stolen. Morality, love, belief in one's self…these things were forever.

Would she say yes?

He would never know if he didn't take the plunge.

"I'd like to see it," he said firmly. "Although I'm not sure I can afford it on a cop's salary."

"They owe you a big raise, if you ask me," Hudson said.

Craig flashed a smile. "Thanks. But it doesn't actually work that way."

"I can give you a price on that ring you can't refuse," Hudson told him.

"I— No, you don't have to."

"Humor me," Hudson said. "Let's honor my dad. The value isn't in the thing, it's in what you do with the thing, remember?"

"Thanks," Craig told him. "Thanks very much."

Twenty minutes later, Craig drove up the Graystones' driveway, parked and got out of his car. He looked up at the sky and shook his head. This was a very different winter, thank God.

It was evening, but he could see the stars. Millions of them. The air was crisp, and there was snow on the ground. It was a beautiful night.

As he headed up the walkway, he could hear the music. Someone was playing the piano—Skyler, he was certain. Frazier's violin and David's rich baritone could be heard.

What a year it had been.

They had never gone back. Just forward.

Life was day to day. You laughed, you cried, you got resentful. You were thrilled, furious, jealous…a million different things. It was different, it was the same. Sometimes there was darkness. And sometimes there were special days, special times. Like Christmas.

He heard Paddy's laughter, followed by Sheila's. They had gotten married six months ago, saying they were both far too old to mess around with a long engagement.

The O'Boyles had wound up keeping the house on Elm, even though at first Skyler had wanted to sell it, would even have given it away.

Kat was the one who had said she wasn't going to allow anyone else's evil to steal what had made her happy. Skyler had thought about that for a while, and in the end they had kept the house, though they had completely redone the kitchen.

Even so, they had decided not to have Christmas Eve dinner there and had gratefully accepted Lydia Graystone's invitation.

As Craig headed toward the door, it opened. And there was Kat, fiery hair blazing in the moonlight, her eyes bright with welcome.

"You're late," she announced, but she was all smiles as she ran into his arms.

He started to speak, to tell her about going by the jewelry store on the way, then decided that could come later.

"Merry Christmas," he said simply. "Merry, merry Christmas."

Turn the page for a preview of
THE DEATH DEALER
the next exciting MIRA Books novel from
New York Times *bestselling author*
Heather Graham.

Look for it in
April 2008
wherever books are sold.

The crash started with what could have been a fender bender, but the first car was pushed into the center lane of the highway, and the driver coming up didn't have time to stop. He slammed hard into the side of the sedan, then careened into the far-left lane.

The car that hit him bounced over the median and into the oncoming traffic.

Joe saw it happen and made it onto the shoulder, threw his car into Park and hit 911 on his cell phone. He reported the accident, dropped the phone and raced over to help.

The smell of gas was strong around the car that had hopped the median.

"Watch out! It's going to go off like a bomb!" someone yelled to Joe as he approached the car. He lifted a hand in acknowledgment and kept going. He was no superhero, but as a cop, he'd worked lots of accident scenes, and an inner voice was assuring him now that he had time.

The car was upside down. There was blood coming from the driver's head, which was resting at an awkward angle. The man's eyes were closed.

"Hey. You have to wake up.... We've got to get you out of there. I'm going to help you," Joe told him.

"My niece," the man said. "You have to help my niece."

The man grabbed Joe, and the strength in his grip was amazing.

Girl? Joe looked into the car, but he didn't see anyone.

"Trish," the man said. "You have to help Trish."

Then Joe saw the little girl. She was in the back. Not really big enough for a seat belt, she had slipped out of it and was on the roof—which was now the floor—with silent tears streaming down her face.

Joe leaned in as far as he could and said coaxingly, "Come on, honey. Give me your hand."

She had huge, saucerlike blue eyes, and was maybe about seven or eight, but tiny for her age, Joe decided. "Trish," he said firmly. "Give me your hand."

He breathed a sigh of relief when she obeyed, and he managed to get her out, even though she had to crawl over broken glass. When he had her in his arms, someone from the milling crowd rushed forward.

"Get the hell out of here, buddy!" a man said urgently as he took the child from Joe's arms. "That car is going to blow."

"There's a man in the car," Joe said.

"He's dead."

"No," Joe said. "He's still alive. He talked to me."

Joe was dimly aware that the evening was alive with sirens—and fully aware that he didn't have much time left before the car caught fire and went up.

Flat on his stomach, he crawled into the car as far as he could.

"Trish," the man in the car said.

"It's all right. She's safe. Now get ready, because I'm releasing the seat belt. Then you've got to try to help me."

He did his best to support the guy's weight after he released the seat belt, though it was a struggle. But he got the man out and could only pray that he hadn't made his injuries worse.

"Help me!" Joe yelled as he began dragging the man as far from the wreck as he could get.

The same good Samaritan who had taken the child came rushing up. Together, they half dragged and half carried the man to the shoulder.

Just in time.

The car exploded, the flames leaping high enough to be seen across the river in Brooklyn.

The blast was hot and powerful. Joe felt it himself, like a huge hand that lifted him, the victim and Joe's fellow rescuer and tossed them across the roadway, then sent them crashing down on the asphalt. He rolled, trying to take the brunt of their landing, knowing he was in far better shape to accept the force than the victim of the crash.

For a moment he couldn't breathe. Then he felt an

ache in every joint, and the hardness of the road against his back. He heard screams all around him, and the shriek of sirens.

"You all right?" he asked the man who had helped him.

"Yeah—you?"

"Fine."

The next thing Joe knew, there was a young EMT hunkering down in front of him as he tried to struggle to his feet.

"Take it easy, sir," the med tech said.

"I'm good," Joe told him. "The guy who helped me—"

"He's being taken care of."

"The man in the car—I think he was hurt pretty badly," Joe said.

"We, uh, we got it," the med tech told him. "And," he added gently, "the little girl is fine. You saved her life."

"Thank God," Joe murmured. "But the man, he—"

"Sir, I'm sorry to tell you, but he's dead."

"Damn. I thought he had a chance."

The med tech was silent for a minute. "You did a

good thing," he said very softly. "But that man…he died on impact. Broken neck."

"No—he talked to me."

"Sir, that man couldn't have spoken to you. I'm sure his family is going to be grateful you got the body out, but he's been dead since the impact. He never suffered."

Joe sat up and stared at the med tech. What did this kid know? He wasn't the coroner.

"He spoke to me. I wouldn't even have seen the kid if he hadn't told me she was in the car. I'm telling you, he was alive."

Of course he'd been alive, Joe told himself. He couldn't have imagined that conversation.

Could he?